1

Copyright

Preface

I've been asked many times how a Bank Director gets an interest in writing a children's fiction story. Let me explain as best I can.

I have had a love of Mull since 1994. My wife, Karen and I enjoyed a day trip where we completed a Wildlife Tour, it was love at first sight with Mull and we've been coming back every year to witness its magic.

I have a passion for Mull, it's an Island with everything, its magnificent scenery, stunning beaches, wildlife in abundance and, in this day and age, it still retains that feeling of stepping back in time when people looked out for one another. I do hope that the Island can retain its magic in the light of increased accessibility and the digital environment.

Above all the tangible aspects of the Island the one thing that makes it truly extraordinary, is the people and since visiting the island we have found some true friends, Muileachs are special people. I am in no way claiming that my book can ever do justice to Mull. What I offer is passion for Mull and all I want to do is to bring some of the beauty of Mull to a few more people through this book.

It has been a real privilege to write this book and I hope that everyone will enjoy reading it as much as I have enjoyed writing it.

For Karen, my loving wife, my daughters Laura and Emma who all share my love of Mull. For all my family and friends who have inspired characters in this book (you know who you are!) and to all the special people of Mull. Thank You!

Contents

Chapter One - Making friends.......

The sun was shining on the remote Scottish Island of Mull. Mull is famous for its white-tailed eagle population and for one particular family of white-tailed eagles called the Muileach family. Generations of Muileachs had lived on Mull for many years; their name meant 'people who come from Mull'.

Mum and Dad Muileach were called Rona and Raasay. They had a young white-tailed eagle called Elgol and they all lived in an area of the island called the 'Tall Trees'. They had chosen this site as it gave them a terrific view of the island, with a clear view out to the west so they could see the changes in the weather as it was approaching, but perhaps, more importantly, it gave them a quiet and safe place to live.

As he grew, Elgol was fed and cared for by both his parents but he was not a helpless chick in the nest for very long. Elgol fledged after a few weeks and was soon old enough to leave the nest. His first task was to learn how to fly. Having watched his parents every day since he was born he didn't think he would ever be able to fly as well as they could. He had marvelled at their skill in flying and how they swooped down to catch prey, but Elgol knew it would be a while yet before he would be able to catch prey with such expertise. He soon mastered how to fly from the nest as far as the rocky mountainside and back to the 'Tall Trees', which was no mean feat especially with the strong westerly winds blowing in. Then tragedy hit.

One bright and sunny morning Raasay went off fishing. He often left the nest before everyone else woke up. It was sometime later that morning that Rona began to worry as Raasay hadn't returned. It wasn't unusual for Raasay to be gone a couple of hours but Rona sensed something was not quite right. Raasay and Rona had been together for many years and she knew his habits very well. This simply did not seem like him.

Not only was Rona aware that something could have happened to Raasay but she was also very aware that it was past Elgol's feeding time and that he was very hungry. Rona told Elgol to stay in the nest and wait until Raasay returned whilst she went fishing. She didn't want to share her worries with Elgol, but she knew, whilst fishing, she would have to go and look for Raasay.

Rona flew off towards their favourite fishing loch where there were plenty of fish, and where she thought she might find Raasay. It didn't take her long to catch a huge salmon, which she knew would satisfy both hers and Elgol's appetite, but there was no sign of Raasay. On her way back, as she flew over the mountain ridge, her eagle eye spotted something strange on the side of the mountain so she swooped down to take a closer look.

There, on the grass by the heather, she could see Raasay. He lay on the ground motionless. Right next to him was a dead sheep. Clearly, there was nothing that she could do to help him and her thoughts returned to Elgol who was all alone back at the nest. She flew as fast as she could with the salmon in her talons, and in no time got back to the nest relieved to see Elgol safe and well but very hungry!

After their meal, Rona sat alongside Elgol in their nest to explain that Dad would not be coming home.

Rona in a quivering voice said 'Elgol, I've got some really sad news to tell you'.

Elgol had enjoyed eating the salmon but sensed his mum's mood change so in a quiet voice said 'What is it Mum? Why are you upset and where's Dad?'

This was really hard for Rona and the hardest thing she'd ever had to do.

She said to Elgol 'When I was flying back from the Loch earlier today I saw your father lying on the mountainside. I am afraid he won't be coming home.' She paused to allow the words that she struggled to speak sink in and then added, 'I'm sorry to say that your father has died.'

Rona could see the shock hitting Elgol as his body started to quiver and tears welled up in his eyes. She placed a wing over him in much the same way that she had done to protect him when he was a tiny chick and they stayed like this for what seemed like an eternity. She slowly pulled her wing away and then said 'I am so sorry Elgol, I think that Dad must have eaten some poisoned meat.'

Elgol was confused and said 'But why would anyone want to hurt Dad?' Rona replied 'I don't think anyone does really, but some farmers, in trying to protect their young lambs, will use poisoned meat.' She added 'Elgol please promise me that you won't eat anything that you suspect has been laid out for bait.'

Elgol could see that it was now time for him to comfort his mum 'Of course I won't Mum, and don't worry I will always be here to protect and look after you.'

Rona knew that, with Raasay now gone, Elgol would have to learn quickly, and that they would have to help each other. The following morning, the serious work began. Elgol felt that he had to step up and take responsibility as he was now head of the family. One of his first tasks was to master the art of fishing as without this skill he wouldn't be able to look after himself let alone help his mum.

Rona decided to teach Elgol straight away, there was no time like the present! They both set off to her favourite fishing loch. This was further than Elgol had been used to flying but Rona knew there would be plenty of fish for Elgol to practise catching.

On their way they encountered a family of gulls. The leader of the pack was called Gus. He was not very nice. The gulls kept dive bombing them and taunting them. Gus said, "What no Raasay today, is he having a lie in?" Little did he know, Rona and Elgol thought, as they flew-off.

When they got to the loch, Rona told Elgol to circle overhead and watch as she fished. Elgol watched his mum circling the loch looking for a suitable fish then suddenly throw her wings back, enter into a steep dive and, with talons out, swoop. She appeared to just skim the water with her talons but she emerged with a large fish in them. Elgol was amazed to see how clever his mum was.

As she flew back up, Elgol could see she had caught an unsuspecting fish. Elgol was so impressed by his mum. She looked so elegant and made it look so easy - he couldn't wait to have a go!

Rona flew back up to Elgol and before she could speak Elgol shouted "That was great Mum. I'm off to have a go, watch me!"

Off he went, circling for a few minutes and then a fish caught his eye glistening in the sunshine. Just like his mum he dived and headed straight for the water. A few feet away from the water and the fish, Elgol got cold feet and decided to pull up. He flapped his wings frantically but, at the speed he was travelling, he slammed into the water. Elgol was completely submerged and swallowed a mouth full of water. He got back to the surface as quickly as he could. Flapping furiously to try and get airborne. He gulped and spluttered as he tried to regain his breath before flying off, wondering how long it would take for his wings to dry out. Meanwhile the fish gently swam away thinking to himself "Another young upstart!"

It didn't take long for Elgol to reach his mum who tried to hide the little smile on her face at watching Elgol's first attempt at fishing as it brought back memories of her own.

'Don't worry.' Rona said 'You'll soon get the hang of it! I think that's enough excitement for one day. We'll try again tomorrow.'

Tomorrow came and the events of the day before were repeated, and the following day, and the next, and the next. Elgol was getting very fed up. In truth Rona was getting worried that Elgol would never get the hang of fishing and would never be able to look after himself. Rona decided to give Elgol a few days off from fishing, hoping that this would take away the pressure that he was feeling. She was sure this was responsible for his continuing failures to catch fish. The last thing she wanted was for Elgol to feel responsible for feeding them both as that was her job.

The next morning Elgol woke up to a beautiful sunny day. Rona said 'Forget about fishing today Elgol. Just go and enjoy yourself, but please stay away from the Dark Cliffs.' These were dangerous places even for white-tailed eagles as in the past there had been rock falls which had destroyed nests. Elgol was quite relieved. He was getting frustrated and feeling the pressure of not catching a fish. With that thought still in his mind off he flew.

After a while, swooping and gliding, Elgol noticed some movement at the side of the loch. Elgol flew down to take a closer look and saw a heron fishing.

Elgol flew about watching the heron intensely and saw that he'd caught a fish – like his Mum, he made it look so easy. Elgol thought to himself - wouldn't Mum be proud of me if I could catch a fish and take it back for supper. He decided he would go and speak to the heron.

"Hello, my name's Elgol and I live in the 'Tall Trees' – what are you doing?" asked Elgol.

"Hello Elgol" the heron replied. "My name's Henry. You must be Raasay's son. I was so sorry to hear what happened to him. No doubt your mum has told you to stay away from farmers and their sheep. I'm fishing, what are you up to today?"

Elgol said, "Yes, she has" with a tear in his eye. "I miss my dad, he was such a good flyer and he taught me how to swoop and dive. Would you teach me how to fish?" asked Elgol.

Henry could see that Elgol was very upset, "Well I could, but you fish differently to how I do it" said Henry.

Elgol pestered Henry and, feeling sorry for him, gave in and agreed.

Henry said "Right, Elgol, stand on that rock over there with your feet just in the water and keep very still. Now watch as a fish swims beneath you and then, quick as lightning, stab your beak in the water and catch the fish."

Henry then showed him how to do it by catching a couple of fish and an eel and swallowing them whole.

Elgol then stood with his feet in the water. He kept perfectly still, as if he was a rock himself. He watched a fish swimming beneath the water and waited......and waited......and waited..... and then he pounced! He felt an excruciating pain in his head and squawked in agony as he missed the fish and hit his beak on a rock! Tears rolled down his face and he could see that the impact on his beak had pushed it out of shape and he now had a crooked beak - what would Mum say!

Henry felt guilty and sent him home saying "I told you that I caught fish differently to you. It's probably best for your mum to teach you to fish in future!"

When Elgol got home his mum could see that something was wrong and, rather embarrassed, Elgol told her what had happened. Rona could see that he'd been forced into fishing this way because of the pressure of not having caught a fish. She said "Don't worry, Elgol, everything will be alright. We'll go fishing again soon." Elgol was not convinced but was more concerned about his aching beak.

The next day Elgol set off again to explore but he promised himself that he wouldn't try fishing today and would also avoid Henry. He was enjoying himself flying around in the sunshine when he saw a young boy who seemed to be skimming stones into the loch. The loch was so still Elgol could see the ripples that they were making. Elgol decided to go and investigate so swooped down to take a closer look.

Elgol landed on some rocks behind the boy and continued watching him and then realised that he wasn't throwing stones at all but small pieces of fish. It became clear that he was actually feeding something in the water. He stared and waited to see what it was, when suddenly a head appeared, grabbed the fish and with a flick of his tail disappeared. No sooner had he done so, a head appeared again and grabbed another piece of fish. This happened several times until Elgol realised that it wasn't one thing eating the fish but two! All this time, Elgol began to get hungry at seeing all these fish and let out a squawk. At this, the boy turned around sharply and the two animals eating the fish disappeared. With the flick of their tails Elgol realised that they were otters.

The boy spoke quietly, "Oh, hello, what's your name?"

"My name's Elgol and I've been watching you feeding those otters." Elgol replied.

"Oh!" said the boy adding "I'm called Callum and these are my two young friends, Olly and Pollyhannah. They are brother and sister otters who live on the loch."

Elgol said "I'm pleased to meet you and I'm so sorry, Callum, for scaring your friends away."

Callum said "Don't worry, they'll soon be back as they haven't finished their lunch yet!"

No sooner had they finished talking than the two otters popped their heads up. They were very shy and nervous as they were still very young - starting to make their way in the big wide world of Mull. They saw Elgol talking to Callum so this gave them confidence.

Olly said "Hi. My name's Olly and this is my sister Pollyhannah. Callum is teaching us how to fish as our Mum and Dad aren't around to show us."

Elgol said "That's a coincidence as I'm learning to fish as well. Where's your Mum and Dad?" Elgol was not prepared for Olly's response when he said "Well, they both died suddenly from a disease and we've been left to fend for ourselves. Thankfully, we met Callum and he's agreed to help us."

Callum then said "They're doing really well and should soon be able to look after themselves." He then added "Sadly, my Mum died last year as well."

Elgol knew exactly how they all felt and said "I'm sorry to hear that. Last week my dad died and I miss him so much." He felt comforted knowing that he still had his Mum.

All afternoon the four of them played together in the water and the time soon came for Elgol to return to the Tall Trees for tea. Before he left, he said to his new friends "Can I come back tomorrow to play and will you teach me how to fish?" Unanimously, they all said "We'd love to!". Elgol left, very excited, and couldn't wait for tomorrow to come.

The next day Elgol got up early and ate the fish his mum had caught for breakfast quickly as he couldn't wait to go down the loch to meet his new friends. When he got there it was very quiet and there was no one to be found. He decided to wait up in a tree. He was there for ages – the only people he saw were some bird watchers who were looking through their binoculars. He even heard them say "Look at that funny bird with the bent beak!"

Not long after they left, he saw Callum coming down the loch in a small rowing boat and he could see him looking up in the sky for Elgol. As he came further down, Elgol flew down to the boat and perched on its side. He could see that Callum was pleased to see him.

Callum said "Where are Olly and Pollyhannah this morning?" Within seconds their heads popped up behind the boat.

Callum had clearly come prepared as Elgol noticed a whole load of fish in the boat. Olly and Pollyhannah swam off and Callum threw fish off the back of the boat.

Olly and Pollyhannah took it in turns to swim up to the surface to catch the fish and thought this was a great game.

Elgol watched intensely and was desperate to have a go. It looked great fun.

Callum said to Elgol "Once you've circled and you're at a decent height I'll throw a fish off the back of the boat. You then swoop down, skim the water with your talons and then fly off with the fish - simple!" This sounded all too familiar thought Elgol, but he was prepared to give it a go if it meant that he could learn to fish.

The plan was hatched and off went Elgol. He circled and circled getting higher and higher with the rowing boat getting smaller and smaller. He then saw a big splash as Callum threw something off the back of the boat.

That was Elgol's trigger to dive, he folded his wings back, went into a steep dive and headed right for the boat - thinking that he was going to hit the boat, he gave up and soared away nowhere near the fish.

Callum shouted to Elgol "The boat's too close to the fish next time I'll row away." They had another go but this time Elgol had forgotten about Olly and Pollyhannah! He swooped down and was just about to grab the fish when Olly swam up beneath the fish and dragged it under leaving Elgol to fly away empty handed. Callum laughed his socks off but Elgol was upset as he still hadn't caught a fish!

Callum had a stern word with Olly and Pollyhannah to leave the fish alone and off Elgol went again. This time everything clicked. It was a perfect dive and pick up and Elgol was chuffed with himself. He swooped down afterwards and shouted to his friends "Thank you!" then off he flew to show his Mum his catch.

Rona was in the tall trees waiting and watching for Elgol. She saw him flying back but had to blink twice as she saw something in his talons, it couldn't possibly be, could it..... could it...... yes it was Elgol carrying a fish!

Rona was so pleased when he returned and was very proud of her son. Elgol didn't have the heart to tell her that he had received a little bit of help along the way!

The next day Rona and Elgol went fishing together and had a wonderful day, each catching fish until they were full. Elgol had finally mastered the art of fishing!

During that summer Elgol mixed up his days with fishing and playing with his friends, although he didn't tell his Mum about them.

A few days later, and on another beautiful sunny morning when Elgol had been fishing, he got back to the Tall Trees and said to his mum "I'm off down the loch to practice my gliding." She said "Take care" and off he went.

He hadn't been down the loch long when he spotted Callum in his rowing boat. He too was fishing with Olly and Pollyhannah.

The weather on Mull was known locally for how quickly it changes and the locals often said "You don't know what the weather is going to do until you look out of the window in the morning". They were so busy fishing that they hadn't noticed the big black clouds rolling down the valley very quickly and, before they knew it, the wind had whipped up into a gale and the boat was rocking fiercely from side to side.

Callum looked frightened when all of a sudden a big wave hit the small boat and both oars fell into the water, Callum made a grab for them and nearly fell into the loch himself. Before he knew it the oars had blown away with no chance of retrieving them. The small boat was being battered by the wind and waves and if Callum was frightened before, he was now terrified. He tried shouting for help but with the wind and rain he knew that nobody would ever hear him.

Elgol had been watching the drama unfold and he saw Olly and Pollyhannah by the side of the boat but he couldn't see how they could possibly help as they themselves were struggling to swim against the wind and waves.

Elgol flew down as best he could and battling against the strong wind and rain. He shouted across to say that he would go to Callum's home to find help and with that off he flew as fast as his wings could flap. Whether they heard him or not he couldn't tell.

Meanwhile Olly and Pollyhannah could see that Callum was in real trouble. In the water they saw the rope that Callum used to tie the boat up with so they both grabbed this in their mouths and started pulling the boat with all their might back towards the shore, although it seemed a very long way off!

Elgol got to Callum's farm and saw his Dad, Ally, trying to get the sheep into a pen as he had seen the storm approaching. Elgol cried as loud as he could to try and make himself heard above the wind but Ally couldn't hear him.

He noticed, though, an old ship's bell outside the farmhouse so, using all his skill that he'd learnt fishing, he swooped down and hit the bell with his talons. The bell swung and made a loud "dong".

This got Ally's attention and he looked up to see the white-tailed eagle. He saw Elgol flying around frantically in circles and a sixth sense told him that something was wrong.

Ally jumped on his quad bike and started following Elgol down the glen. He soon realised that he was heading to the loch and that this was where Callum had told him he was going.

As he followed Elgol, the wind was howling and it was raining very strongly. It had also gone very dark as if it was night-time. He would never forgive himself if anything had happened to Callum. Ally, fearing the worst, started to panic and he pushed the quad bike to go as fast as it could. The path was rocky and very slippery and there were several times that Ally thought the quad bike would tip over but he kept going.

He got to the edge of the loch and looked out across the water as best he could. He spotted the small rowing boat and realised that it was Callum's. He shouted to Callum but he couldn't hear him. Looking at the boat he couldn't understand how the boat was making its way towards the shore as Callum was waving with both arms. Ally jumped off the quad bike and ran down to the water's edge shouting to the boat "Callum, Callum!"

Ally then ran into the water and was up to his waist by the time he reached the boat. As he waded closer, he saw two exhausted otters clutching the rope to the boat in their teeth and he realised that they had dragged the boat to safety and saved his son's life.

Ally got everyone safely ashore. Callum and Ally gave Elgol a huge wave and, with that, Elgol headed back home to tell his Mum about his huge adventure.

Ally gave Callum a huge hug. It was clear that the two otters, Olly and Pollyhannah, were really struggling. Callum was worried that the rescue had been too much for them. They were very weak and their breathing was very shallow. There was a wooden box with a sack inside on the back of the quad bike in which they carefully placed Olly and Pollyhannah. They then made their way back to the farm-house where Callum watched over them until they arrived.

At the farmhouse, Ally took Callum into the warm kitchen where they gave Olly and Pollyhannah some warm milk and fresh fish.

Meanwhile, in the Tall Trees, Rona had become worried about Elgol as he'd been gone a long time and the weather was atrocious.

She had waited anxiously, not knowing whether she should go out and look for him, but decided the best thing to do was to wait in the trees - she just hoped that he was strong enough to fly through the gales or had the sense to take cover. She was on the point of flying off to find Elgol when she saw him returning looking very ragged and windswept. He flew down and perched on the branch beside her where he told her all about his friends, the storm, the farmer and how he had saved them all. Rona was very proud of her son and thought how very much like his father he had become.

Back at the farmhouse it wasn't long before Olly and Pollyhannah had regained their strength and as the days passed they started to make themselves feel at home. The farm cats disappeared, preferring to keep out of the way and their dogs were so fed up of having their tails bitten that they spent all their time in their baskets. Olly and Pollyhannah enjoyed running in and out of the kitchen and playing with all the laundry in the wash basket, all much to Callum's amusement.

Once the storm had died down, Callum and his dad took Olly and Pollyhannah back to the loch and let them go where they swam off to their holt for a well-earned rest.

Back home Ally was listening to Callum telling his friends on the telephone the story of how the otters and white-tailed eagle had saved his life. Oh, how he wished he could be telling this to his wife, who had sadly passed away last year following a serious illness. Ally knew, though, that his wife would be looking down on Callum and he was convinced that she had kept him safe. On hearing the story again his Dad was moved to tears.

Over the following days, Ally realised just how much he owed to the white-tailed eagle who had alerted him to the danger that Callum was in. He thought that perhaps white-tailed eagles aren't the pests that he had once thought they were. Ally decided that he wanted to do more on the island to educate other farmers and islanders about the wonders of the wildlife on their door-step.

Ally applied for, and became, the Wildlife Warden for the island. He used the story of Olly, Pollyhannah and, of course, Elgol, the famous fisherman of Mull in the schools to help educate the children all across the Island.

Chapter Two - Mission K

After Elgol's adventure saving Callum from the storm, life got back to normal and Elgol spent the rest of the summer practising his fishing and flying skills.

It was one of the warmest and sunniest summers for many years on Mull and Elgol was very happy playing with his new friends and spending time with his Mum.

With all the fish he had been eating, Elgol was now nearly adult size. He had also become more confident and was starting to spread his wings and fly further afield. He soon got to know other White-tailed eagles on the island. He got on particularly well with a family called the Kilbeg's and with their daughter Ella. Ella was the same age as Elgol and they spent many hours together. One of their favourite games was annoying the gulls.

The gulls spent a lot of their time on the seashore by the local fish farm, as there was plenty of food there. They seemed to be eating all the time - with what they ate, Elgol often wondered how they ever got off the ground!

The gulls were good at being annoying birds, especially to the workers at the fish farm - but they were quite nervous, especially at the time of year when they had just had their chicks. Every time a White-tailed eagle flew too close to them they would take to the skies, worried that one of the White-tailed eagles would swoop down and eat them or, worse still, one of their chicks.

Ella and Elgol soon worked this out, so for fun, every day they would always make a point of flying over the fish farm so that they could see all the gulls taking to the air in panic only to return to the seashore five minutes later to continue feeding. One day in August they managed to get the gulls to take to the air over twenty times - it is fair to say that these hungry birds soon became angry birds!

White-tailed eagles on the island are quite the celebrities as people come from far and wide to see these magnificent birds flying. The highlight for any birdwatcher would be to watch a white-tailed eagle catch a fish.

Rona and Elgol were the most popular white-tailed eagles on Mull for several reasons - they flew every day, they lived in an accessible place, they even had a CCTV camera on their nest and finally, Elgol was very recognisable because of his crooked beak.

Because of the CCTV camera, Rona and Elgol were quite friendly with Callum's dad Ally who was now the Wildlife Warden on Mull - it was his job to protect their nest and look after them.

During the summer Ally arranged visits for tourists to visit the white-tailed eagle bird hide, where birdwatchers could look at the nest through powerful telescopes or binoculars. They could even watch the nest on the television from the CCTV that had been set up near the nest. Elgol and Rona quite liked the fame of being on TV and were thinking of auditioning for a talent show to display their fishing skills – all they needed to do now was to learn to sing and play the bagpipes!

Rona and Elgol were amazed at just how many people wanted to visit the hide and they often put on a show for the tourists by fishing and doing some acrobatics. Elgol's party piece was moving his head from side to side in a dance type movement in time to rap music that he once heard on someone's phone down the loch. This really amused the visitors, especially the children.

Ally and the other Wildlife Wardens, together with local residents, did a great job of protecting the white-tailed eagles. Rona and Elgol always felt happy and secure in their nest.

Now, not a lot of people know this, but in addition to the white-tailed eagle's incredible eyesight they have excellent hearing. One sunny day, Ally was showing some visitors to the bird hide. Elgol was flying back to the nest, minding his own business, when he saw around half a dozen people heading into the hide. He felt it strange that two people seemed to be hanging back whispering to each other and continually looking over their shoulders.

Elgol returned to the nest where his Mum was enjoying her lunch. Elgol said "I've just seen two strange men acting suspiciously down by the bird-hide."

Rona replied, "I always think that birdwatchers in general are pretty strange – they travel miles, sit for hours on end looking into the sky, have something to eat, sleep and then start all over again!"

Elgol then said thoughtfully, "Isn't that exactly what we do - we must be pretty strange as well then!" They both then chuckled to themselves.

Elgol couldn't get the two people out of his head so decided that, when they left the hide, he would follow them as he was sure that they were up to no good. After about an hour, the people left the hide and with that Elgol took off from the nest.

He watched the two men head back to their van which was parked about half a mile through the forest. They didn't hang around and drove off. Elgol decided to follow them.

They went about three miles then pulled over on the shore of the loch where they had pitched their tents. Elgol could also see two canoes by the tents. There seemed to be something strange but Elgol couldn't think what. He sat and watched for ages (he was good at this!) and then suddenly he worked out what was so strange.

The island attracts many canoeists over the summer as it provides safe and exhilarating canoeing around the lochs and inlets and, apart from flying like a white-tailed eagle, it's probably the best way to see the island. Elgol had seen many canoes before but only bright coloured ones, so they could be easily spotted at sea but for some reason these were painted black. He thought this was very strange as it made them look sinister and Elgol was suspicious.

Elgol watched and waited but couldn't spot anything wrong and was now feeling very tired. He decided that he would need some help in watching these guys as he was convinced that something wasn't right. With this in mind, he thought that Ella, Olly, Pollyhannah and Callum would love to help him on his investigation.

Elgol flew off and called a meeting of his friends at his favourite place which was under a quiet secluded bridge on the edge of the loch, at 7 o'clock that evening.

Everyone was excited about being called to this secret meeting and couldn't possibly think what it could be about.

Elgol arrived, having got there early, and one by one his friends arrived - Olly and Pollyhannah were first, having spent their day playing tricks on tourists by pretending to be seals.

Ella arrived next, having enjoyed an adventurous day helping her parents re-build their nest following damage caused by strong winds the previous night.

Callum was the last to arrive and he was quite envious as he'd had the most boring day...... at school! All of them had one thing in common; they were all intrigued as to why Elgol had called them all together.

Elgol told everyone what he had seen and about his concerns. Olly and Pollyhannah didn't see too much wrong with what Elgol had seen, although they did think the black canoes were odd. Callum and Ella agreed with Elgol that these guys were up to something. Olly and Pollyhannah were outnumbered but agreed to help anyway.

Elgol said "These guys need watching to see what they are up to." He then hatched a plan for them to take it in turns to watch them every single minute - day and night!

Tomorrow was Saturday so Callum could help out in the day once he'd done his chores on the farm. Olly and Pollyhannah would take the night watch and Elgol and Ella would do the rest between them. They all left excited about the adventure they were about to embark on. Elgol took the first watch.

He sat up in an old fir tree high above the loch and looked down as the two young men, dressed in camouflage jackets, tucked into their supper, having cooked it on an open fire. As the smoke drifted up to the tree where Elgol was sitting he could tell it was mackerel and he suddenly became very hungry and realised he hadn't eaten all day having been too wrapped up in the day's excitement. The men spoke quietly, but not too quiet as Elgol could hear every word.

They talked about the white-tailed eagles, one said "How many nests are there on the island?" Elgol didn't hear the reply but he could see them with a map and that they were putting a cross on it. He could also see that there were several other crosses on the map.

Once they had finished their supper they opened a box of outdoor gear - boots, ropes, harnesses, life jackets - and spent an hour checking them over.

Afterwards, Elgol heard them talking again. "Goodnight" the one said with the other replying "Goodnight, we need an early start in the morning – see you at 5.30.".

With that it all went quiet and Elgol decided to find Olly and Pollyhannah to tell them that he was heading home to get some sleep and that it was their turn to watch the two men.

Olly and Pollyhannah found a nice smooth rock close to the tents and settled down together, particularly as it was getting cold. It wasn't long before they both fell fast asleep - so much for keeping watch!

As soon as the sun came up though, it was a different story and they both sprang into life. They woke up feeling very hungry, looked at the tents and as there was no sign of life they decided to go fishing, both promising to be as quiet as they could so as not to disturb the men in their tents.

After about half an hour, and having eaten several crabs, they saw that there was movement outside the tents. One of the men called out "Charlie!" in a whispering shout. "What is it Bob?" He replied in a loud voice. "Shhhhhh" he said, "look, two otters fishing."

They grabbed their binoculars and crawled along the seashore to get a closer look. They hid behind a large rock and continued watching Olly and Pollyhannah.

Olly and Pollyhannah thought this was great - they were supposed to be watching Charlie and Bob, yet they were watching them! Olly and Pollyhannah then thought actually this was the best way of keeping tabs on them, so they carried on fishing and playing. After a while Charlie and Bob started talking about their day ahead.

Charlie said "We'll load up the canoes and then paddle round the Dark Cliffs."

Bob replied excitedly "I've got the replacement eggs to fool those stupid birds."

Olly and Pollyhannah were confused, but between them, decided that they would report back to Elgol. They swam away to find Elgol, leaving Charlie and Bob cooking a bacon and sausage breakfast on their camp fire.

Elgol was talking to Callum, who had got up early to do his chores so that he could spend the rest of his day on more exciting things. Olly and Pollyhannah arrived and told them what they had heard;

none of them could understand what it all meant but now all agreed that there were sinister plans afoot.

Callum hid himself away up the glen watching the tents with some binoculars that he'd borrowed from his Dad earlier that morning. His Dad had thought that he was going to use them to watch a family of buzzards; little did he know that he was using them to watch a different type of prey!

Callum saw them pack their canoes and head off down the loch and around the Dark Cliffs. It was now lunchtime so Callum handed over to Ella to continue the watch. It would be much easier for her to keep track of the men now that they were on the move.

Callum arrived home to find his Dad was writing up his monthly warden's report. He asked Callum if he'd had a good morning.

Callum replied "Yes Dad, I've been watching two crooks who've been planning a raid!" Ally thought that Callum was talking about the buzzards!

Over lunch, they talked about the white-tailed eagles and Callum asked "Dad, why are there CCTV cameras on the white-tailed eagles' nest?"

His Dad explained "It's to let people have a better view of the birds so they can appreciate them more, but they're also there to protect the birds."

Callum was confused. "Why do they need protecting?" He asked his Dad.

Ally replied "White-tailed eagles are rare and there are some people who are thieves and would steal the white-tailed eagles' eggs. They are very valuable and can be sold for thousands of pounds."

Callum nearly choked on his sandwich as he suddenly realised what Charlie and Bob were up to but he couldn't tell his Dad as, without proof, he didn't think he would believe him.

Callum had never eaten his lunch quicker and was soon on his bike to go and look for Elgol.

Callum found Elgol who was talking to Ella. She was quite upset as she realised that the two men had been heading in the direction of the family nest where her mother had just laid another two eggs. Ella was worried about her family.

Ella had been so excited about the prospect of having another sister or, hopefully a brother and a sister. She was convinced it would be one of each. Callum was desperate to interrupt their conversation as he knew what the two men were up to. He couldn't get his words out quick enough and, in truth, Elgol and Ella couldn't understand a word that he was saying. Elgol told him to take a deep breath, slow down and start again!

Callum repeated the conversation he'd had with his Dad about the robbers who stole white-tailed eagle eggs. Callum was convinced that this was exactly what Charlie and Bob were up to. They all agreed but what could they do to stop them?

Callum said "We need to get proof. If I tell my Dad he will go and tackle them, then they'll just run away and could end up stealing eggs somewhere else."

They all agreed that they couldn't let this happen. Ella was even more frightened now as she realised that the brother and sister that she'd been looking forward to for all this time were under threat and she wanted to warn her parents.

Elgol comforted her and said "I won't let anything bad happen to you or your family. Trust me.' Ella felt reassured and believed that Elgol would protect her. Elgol then took to the skies to find out where the two robbers were and to keep an eye on them.

He soon found them in their canoes floating by the shore and as he got closer he could see that they were looking up through their binoculars at the Kilbeg's nest. He also saw them with a high powered camera taking lots of photographs.

After about half an hour a fishing boat came around the headland and Elgol recognised this as one of the boats from the pontoon returning from a fishing trip to Iona.

The two men in canoes also saw it and, as quick as a flash, they turned their canoes around, hid their cameras and binoculars, and took out some fishing rods starting to use them to fish.

To the people on the boat they just appeared to be adventurous fishermen. If Elgol wasn't convinced that they were up to no good before, then he was now!

Once the fishing boat was out of sight the two men packed up their rods and headed back to shore and Elgol heard Charlie say "We're on for tonight, provided the weather's right." Elgol now knew that time was against them and he had to work out a plan to stop them stealing the eggs.

Elgol got his friends together at 5 o'clock at their bridge and told them what he had planned for that evening and to make sure everyone was clear on their jobs for "Mission K" - the mission to protect the Kilbeg nest. They were all excited, even if a little bit scared. Knowing what they had to do, they went away to get some food and prepare for what was going to be a long night ahead.

Callum went home and went to bed as normal but this was anything but a normal night. Rather than put his pyjamas on he went to bed in his clothes and had prepared a ruck-sack full of provisions to sustain him for a long night out by the loch. His pack included binoculars, one of his Dad's walkie-talkies, some rope, a bar of chocolate and a camera - in fact everything that your average spy would take with him on a mission.

He set his alarm to go off on vibrate at 11 o'clock, normally this would have woken him but on this occasion it didn't as he was already awake, excited and nervous at what lay ahead.

Callum got out of bed, gathered his ruck-sack and sneaked out of the farmhouse, being careful not to wake the farm dogs. When he was far enough away from the house he jumped on his bike to cycle down the loch to meet his friends.

He arrived at Elgol's favourite meeting place about 1/4 mile away from where they'd left the men's tent earlier that evening and waited for the others. It was so dark, and he heard so many noises that he was unfamiliar with - it made him feel like this was not such a good idea after all.

It wasn't long before he heard the familiar high squeaks and recognised this to be Olly and Pollyhannah. He had never been so pleased to see them - then he thought, oh yes he had, when they had rescued him in the storm.

They all waited until Elgol and Ella appeared. Ella, though, had some bad news. As she was flying to the bridge down the loch, she noticed that the tent and canoes had all gone and that there was no sign of the van. Could all this have been for nothing and the men had taken off empty handed? Could they have worked out Elgol's plan to catch them?

They had mixed emotions. On the one hand they were all a bit relieved, but, on the other hand they were all disappointed as their evening adventure seemed to be drawing to an end. Elgol said that he would fly down the loch to take a closer look.

It didn't take long for Elgol to reach where they had camped and, as Ella had reported, everything was gone. Elgol though, had a sixth sense that everything wasn't quite as it seemed so he decided to fly a bit further down the loch. A movement caught his eye under the Dark Cliffs and he could see the two canoes slowly making their way to the Kilbeg's nest. Elgol turned around and started flying back to his friends but on his way he noticed something glistening in the moonlight under some bushes. He flew down to take a closer look and saw that it was Charlie's van hidden beneath a makeshift camouflage net. Mission K was still clearly on!

Elgol reported back to his friends what he had seen and told everyone "Mission K is on; you all know what you need to do!"

Callum's job was to watch where the men had been camping. He thought this was going to be easy but his first job was going to be to find the van!

Ella was to observe the canoes and to keep an eye on them whilst Olly and Pollyhannah followed them from a safe distance. It was now all systems go.

Charlie and Bob made their way around the Dark Cliffs. It had taken a lot longer than it had done earlier that day as the wind had got up and paddling was very hard, but they edged ever closer and closer to the nest.

With every stroke of the paddle, Ella became more and more nervous as to what might happen and she didn't know what plans Elgol had to stop them. She just knew that she had to trust Elgol.

After about an hour, the canoes pulled up on the shore by the Kilbeg's nest. Charlie and Bob unloaded the canoes. They had a steep climb of several hundred feet to get to the fir trees where the nest was and then they would have to climb up the tree about forty feet to reach the nest to get the eggs. Elgol watched as they took a drink out of a flask to keep out the cold. They then started climbing up the steep bank, fully laden with ruck-sacks and ropes, looking quite funny with headlamps on which made them appear as if they'd only got one eye!

Elgol thought to himself "There's only one thing that you are up to and you aren't wardens!' With that thought, Elgol flew off.

Ella was watching from trees by their nest and she was shocked to see Elgol fly off. She thought, "Surely he can't be deserting me and my family in our hour of need?" She was really torn as to whether to fly after him or stay. She remembered his words that he would protect her, and to trust him, she just hoped that he was telling the truth.

It didn't take long for Elgol to reach the shore by the fish farm and there, settled down for the night, were all the gulls. Quite a bunch of hooligans - herring gulls, black-headed gulls, lesser black backed and, even an Icelandic gull that had been blown off course by the strong winds earlier in the week. Elgol shouted down to the leader, a Great Black-Backed Gull called Gus "You remember our conversation earlier - we're on, Mission K is a go!"

With that all the gulls took to the air. The sky was a mass of flying wings - it's amazing that no one crashed into one another. In the middle of them was a poor little Icelandic gull, who didn't know which day of the week it was, but, nevertheless thought it looked like fun, so went along anyway.

When Elgol returned to the nest he saw that Charlie and Bob had made quicker progress than he had thought or hoped. They had reached the trees and were already half way up the tree where Ella's family nest was.

Ella's mum and dad had heard the commotion but didn't want to leave the nest as they wanted to protect the eggs. Their first thought was that someone was trying to cut their tree down but they knew that forestry workers or bird-ringers don't work at night; they were so confused and frightened.

Elgol could see that time was against them. He signalled to Gus who yelled out an order "Dive, dive, dive!!"

Leading the way, Elgol went into a steep dive and, with over a hundred gulls following him, they headed straight for Charlie and Bob. One by one they attacked Charlie and Bob by squawking and pooing on them. Ella was circling overhead and could see everything that was going on. She was amazed at the accuracy of the gulls' bombs and it didn't take long for Charlie and Bob's dark camouflaged coats to turn white!

Charlie and Bob were getting very flustered as they were pelted time after time. Charlie lost his footing and ended upside down in the tree. Just as he let out a yelp, the noise was quickly muffled as he received a full mouthful of Icelandic gull poo, which can't have been nice!

Bob shouted down "This is hopeless, let's get out of here, it's not worth it for a couple of eggs, no matter how rare!" With that Charlie and Bob scampered down the tree as fast as they could. At the bottom they quickly packed up their things but they didn't realise that, as they rushed away, their two bobble hats fell out of the ruck-sack.

They got back to their canoes and started paddling away. Ella who had been watching all the action was still chuckling to herself as she saw the two canoes spinning away looking like they were being powered by two cake whisks.

The gulls retreated and Elgol went to Gus, the ringleader, and said "Thank you."

Gus said "Don't forget your promise." Elgol had promised Gus that whenever Ella and he were flying they would give the seashore by the fish farm a wide berth so that the gulls could feed uninterrupted.

Elgol replied "I haven't forgotten."

To a large extent, Olly and Pollyhannah had missed all the action but it was now their turn to follow Charlie and Bob. This time they were finding it quite hard to keep up with them, but they did. After Charlie and Bob had been paddling for a while they began to slow as they were getting tired. It soon became clear that they were heading back to their campsite so Olly agreed to swim on ahead to warn Callum that they were on their way back.

All this time, Callum had been tucked up behind some rocks watching the van and the shore with a million thoughts going through his mind. "What if they hadn't been able to stop them; what if one of his friends had got hurt; what if they had in fact given up, what if...?"

Suddenly, with a splish-splash, out popped Olly from the water and with a quick shake of his fur he headed for Callum. Although he couldn't see him, he could smell him.

Olly said "We don't have a lot of time. Charlie and Bob are right behind me heading back to the van and they haven't got the eggs so they're not in a great mood!"

Straight away, Callum got on the walkie-talkie to his Dad to let him know what was going on but no matter how hard he tried, no one answered from home. He couldn't understand why his Dad didn't answer. Callum was starting to panic. What could he do? He decided the only thing was to try and slow them down somehow.

Olly started making this weird noise quietly "Phshhhh, phshhhh." Callum realised that Olly wanted him to let down the tyres on the van. Quickly, he started letting down the tyres and was on the second one when he could hear splashing from the loch. It was Charlie and Bob back on the shore. Callum slipped away silently back behind his rock so they didn't see him, wondering what to do next.

Meanwhile Olly slipped back into the water to find Pollyhannah.

Charlie and Bob started packing the van as quickly as they could and had decided to catch the first ferry in the morning back to the mainland. They hadn't got long as it was already getting light and they still had quite a drive. No time for a leisurely breakfast this morning. Once they'd packed up they removed the branches hiding the van and they were about to head off when they noticed that two of the tyres were flat. Blaming each other and grumbling away, they got the pump from the back of the van and inflated the tyres.

Callum felt helpless, he was all alone and there was nothing that he could do to stop them. The nest robbers set off down the road around the loch and headed towards the ferry.

When they had gone a safe distance, Callum emerged from his hiding place quite distraught that he hadn't been able to stop the robbers. He then saw Duncan the local game-keeper coming along the road in his familiar Land-rover. Duncan was from the local estate and a friend of his father and he was surprised to see Callum in the middle of the road. Duncan stopped and asked Callum "What are you doing out and about so early in the morning?"

Callum told him the whole story. Duncan then said "I became suspicious yesterday when I saw them as I was coming back on the fishing boat from Iona. I felt something was wrong when I saw them fishing in an area that no recognised fisherman would ever fish."

Callum said "I can't get hold of my Dad." It soon became clear why not.

Duncan said "I raised my concerns with your Dad as the local warden and we both went out last night to watch the Kilbeg's nest. Laura, from the coffee shop had come round to stay at the farm to keep an eye on you. Clearly, she didn't do a great job!"

Duncan went on "We saw exactly what was happening but, from afar. We were in a remote area and there was no walkie-talkie signal. Your Dad stayed to guard the nest and I left to tell the police. It's taken me a lot longer to get around the loch than canoeing as it's a lot further and some of the road has been washed away because of the recent storms."

Duncan said "Jump in, Callum, I've got something to show you!"

With that, Callum got into the Land-rover. All this time, Elgol and Ella had been watching Callum and decided to follow Duncan. It soon became clear that he was heading to the ferry terminal.

They arrived just in time to see Charlie and Bob being put into the back of the police van to be taken away for questioning.

The 'Mission K' team all felt very proud of themselves as they had stopped this horrible crime and they had saved the Kilbeg family. In fact, Ella went on to have a brother called Rhys and a sister Eva, and they all became great friends.

They were all pleased that Charlie and Bob would never again steal eggs - even from a supermarket! Of course the robbers denied the whole event but no one believed them as they had white smelly camouflage jackets and, when it was proven that the bobble hats found at the crime scene belonged to Charlie and Bob, they were found out as their names were on labels inside!

Callum became quite the local hero when news got out about the arrests and he even got his picture in the local newspaper. Callum did feel a little guilty of receiving all the attention for single-handedly beating the egg stealers. Little did they know, he thought!

In the meantime, his friends looked on proudly thinking "We can't wait for our next adventure........."

Chapter Three - Competition comes to Mull

Mull is famous for two things, Balamory the town with painted houses from the popular Children's TV programme and the other being the wide and diverse wildlife that is seen on the island throughout the year. Both have attracted lots of visitors to the island but perhaps one more than the other!

Callum had spent the morning at Elgol's favourite place playing with his friends – Elgol, Ella, Olly and Pollyhannah. They had been skimming, fishing and generally having a good time.

Callum left them to cycle home along the road by the loch. This was a single track road and popular with wildlife watchers hoping to see a glimpse of an otter or a white-tailed eagle.

He got so far when he noticed a commotion on the road. There was a Land-rover and a mini-bus blocking the road which looked very strange. As he got closer he could see that both were full of passengers, clearly both on wildlife-watching tours as they all had binoculars around their necks. Both vehicles had reached a point in the road where it was impossible for them to pass - certainly not without one of them getting stuck in a ditch. They had reached a 'Mexican stand-off' with both drivers refusing to back up. As Callum got closer, he could hear raised voices out of the window each telling the other person to back up. There was then an argument as to who was closer to the last passing place with each contending that the other was closer. The voices became louder and louder and they became more and more animated - at this, both sets of passengers were also getting agitated, as they were fearful that they were going to miss their ferry back to Oban. It was clear that neither driver was in any mood to back down and both got out of their vehicles. As they did, one of the passengers also emerged from the Land-rover.

he man said pompously, "My name is Marcus Robertson-Smythe and I'm a solicitor from Gatward and McCallum, Solicitors." He added "There's only one way to solve this dispute." Speaking to the two drivers he asked them "Do you agree to me sorting out this matter? If you do, then we can get this matter resolved in next to no time and we can get back to enjoying our tour." Callum looked on with interest.

Reluctantly both drivers agreed.

Marcus then said "Whoever is nearest to the last passing place needs to back up. Agreed?" This seemed a reasonable compromise as both thought that they were furthest away! They both went back to their respective vehicles and paced it out back to the passing place. They returned to Marcus and the first driver said "Its 26 paces." The other said "Its 28."

Marcus adjudicated and told the first driver "You're 26 paces so you need to back up." Simple, or so he thought!

The second driver though argued "I'm 6 inches taller than him and therefore I've got bigger paces, I demand a recount!"

After some further discussion it was agreed that Marcus would pace it out, which he did, and came to the same decision. Whilst grumbling under his breath, the driver closest to the passing place returned to his vehicle and backed up - Callum thought he had never seen anyone reverse more slowly in all his life!

The most amusing thing about all of this was that Callum's friends had heard the commotion and had come down the loch to see what was going on. Elgol and Ella were flying over the vehicles and Olly and Pollyhannah were sat out on a rock watching with amusement. With everything going on, not one of the wildlife-watchers spotted them. If they had, they would have had the best view of their lives!

Callum was still smiling when he got back home thinking how silly adults could be sometimes and maybe **they** should get their pocket money stopped!

That afternoon, Callum helped his Dad on the farm collecting in some bales of hay. It was warm work, and after a while they stopped for a drink of lemonade. Callum thought back to the times when his Mum would bring them drinks to the field and a small tear started rolling down his cheek. How he missed her.

Callum took the opportunity during the break to tell his Dad what he'd seen down the loch earlier that day.

Ally smiled when he heard the story but he said to Callum "As wildlife warden on the island, I'm getting quite concerned about the number of tours taking place around the island and the effect that they are having on the wildlife."

He admitted that he didn't quite know what to do about it. This gave Callum food for thought and he decided to talk to his friends about this later as clearly they were affected.

Wildlife tours had started on the island twenty-five years ago, not long after white-tailed eagles had been re-introduced. At that time, there were only two tours – 'Wildlife Extravaganzas' run by Douglas MacDougall, who had been brought up on the island and knew every square inch of it and 'Awesome Mull' run by Alex and Gemima Bird. They had moved to the island from London where they'd been accountants but wanted to get out of the rat race.

At this time, they both got on with each other very well. They helped each other by sharing information as to what wildlife was about and there was plenty of business to go around. Over the years though, as more and more people realised what an idyllic place Mull was to live, more and more people had moved to the island and others had bought a mini-bus and set themselves up as wildlife tour operators.

There were now ten on the island, each claiming to be the best, the longest established, the most successful, the cheapest. All in all, competition was fierce and the rivalry intense. All of them even claimed to serve the best scones on the island when everyone knew that Laura's at the Coffee Shop were the best, not only on Mull but in Scotland!

As time went on, Ally could see that there would be more and more incidents like Callum had witnessed earlier today. Only last week another tour operator had set up "SAYSF" Tours - it took Ally ages to work out that SAYSF stood for "Seek and Ye Shall Find".

Later that day Callum was talking to his friends and telling them about the incident on the road. Altogether they replied "We know, we were there!" They all decided that something needed to be done about them as so many tours were making their life difficult.

Olly said "I nearly got run over when a tour guide was looking out over the loch whist I was crossing the road."

Pollyhannah added "I don't get any peace and don't feel safe sleeping on the seashore rocks anymore."

Elgol said "I'm still worried about people stealing eggs."

They all suggested ideas, none of which they thought would work.

All of a sudden, Callum shouted "I've got it!"

His friends nearly jumped out of their skins. Callum said "The only way to solve who has the best wildlife tour is to hold a competition for all of the tour operators on the island. We could get them all together at the start of the day and then send them off to see who can record the most number of different species of wildlife during the day. The operator who records the highest number will be crowned the winner." He went on, "To support the wildlife, the tour operators can gather sponsorship for every record gathered - the recording will be judged by a couple of recognised wildlife experts from the island."

They all thought it was a brilliant idea and Callum rode off home on his bike as fast as his legs would pedal to tell his Dad his idea.

He didn't really think his Dad would share his enthusiasm but, surprisingly, he also thought it was a terrific idea and that it would bring some focus back on the wildlife of Mull and not be just about making money.

Ally set about contacting all of the operators. One or two were a bit sceptical as they couldn't see anything in it for them but once they realised that others had agreed to "compete" he soon had everyone signed up.

They agreed a date and they all set about getting sponsors for the big event. Callum and his friends were looking forward to the event as well and they were as excited as everyone else.

By the time the day of the competition arrived sponsorship money of over £1,000 had been raised. Ally was very pleased as he was going to share this money between the Bird Conservation Society and The Otter Salvation Fund who were going to use the money to erect some road signs to tell drivers to slow down and some special reflective poles.

Everyone gathered at Laura's famous Coffee Shop on Mull where they shared a bacon baguette. I think that alone would have been enough to get people to participate as everyone would travel miles for one of Laura's bacon baguettes!

They all wolfed down their food and couldn't wait to get started as they had to be back at the Coffee Shop by 5 o'clock to hand in their results.

Off they went, all sprinting to their vehicles to get off to a flying start. They all wanted to win and be crowned the 'Best Wildlife Tour' on Mull.

Callum and his friends were all watching from down the loch. Olly and Pollyhannah stayed there all day and did their best to keep out of sight as they didn't want to make life easy for anyone. Elgol and Ella flew all over the island keeping an eye on the vehicles circling the island. Elgol said to Ella "Look, they all look like little ants running around!"

It was a tiring day for all concerned and the tension was at fever pitch by the time they all got back to the Coffee Shop at 5 o clock. The senior wildlife watcher on the island was Douglas MacDougall - everyone thought that he would win. He seemed to have a sixth sense about where the wildlife would be and his eyesight was superb - no wonder they nicknamed him "Eagle Eye".

You could imagine everyone's surprise when the results were reported. They were announced in reverse order and the tension was really mounting as it got down to the last two scores to be announced.

Ally said "In second place.............. with 93 species, is........... Douglas MacDougall" Then shock horror as he said "With 98 species in first place are "SAYSF" Tours!"

Everyone was flabbergasted, other than the people from "SAYSF" tours who were declared the winner and accepted with a smug look on their faces. Douglas demanded a recount but even after this they still won - clearly he was not happy!

Now, Callum, who had been listening to the results, overheard the couple from SAYSF Tours talking as they made their way back to their car. The man said to his wife, "It just shows that preparation pays!"

Callum thought this was a strange comment to make and became suspicious, sensing another adventure on its way!

Callum got to their regular meeting place where all his friends were waiting for him to report back the results - they couldn't wait and were very excited.

They, too, were amazed to hear that "Eagle Eye" hadn't won as they all thought it was going to be a foregone conclusion. They were surprised about "SAYSF" as none of them had heard of them. When

Callum told them about what he'd overheard they agreed it sounded suspicious.

Callum told them that he would get hold of the records to see if there was anything fishy going on.

With the mention of fish, Olly said "I'm hungry and need to find a crab quickly!"

They agreed to meet the following day to see what Callum had found out.

That night, Callum went through the record sheets. On them had been recorded what was seen, when and where. All looked in order and he read the records many times over as he was desperate to find something wrong - he was convinced that there was a problem but just couldn't see it.

He decided to have his tea and study them again later.

Straight after tea he picked up the "SAYSF" sheet and spotted it straight away and thought "how silly am I?" On line 56 it showed that a magpie had been spotted down Loch Scridian by the car park - this was it, he'd found the error!

The following day, he got up early and headed to meet his friends at their meeting place down their loch, keen to show his friends what he'd found.

"There" Callum said, "Line 56 - the Magpie"

"So what?" Said Olly.

None of them could understand the significance of line 56. How could they have missed it! Callum explained what was staring them all in the face "Magpies on Mull are so rare I find it hard to believe that someone saw one yesterday."

They agreed to check the whole list out to see if they could find anything else wrong by visiting the place of each sighting. They split the list up, with Elgol and Ella checking the inaccessible places and Olly and Pollyhannah the seashore birds. They agreed to meet back again at the bridge at four o'clock and off they went. Olly and Pollyhannah set off down Loch Scridian to find the heron.

They got to the place to where the heron was recorded and didn't really expect to see anything, but there, on the rock exactly where it had been recorded, was the heron. He was as still as anything and they both thought that he was fishing so left him alone and went to look for the two oystercatchers which were next on the list.

They soon found these exactly where they were recorded on the list - they both remarked that this bird watching was a piece of cake. Further down the loch they saw the curlew again where it should be.

Off they went again, when they saw the sandpipers they knew that something wasn't right.

Everyone knows that sandpipers continually bob up and down but this one was as still as a statue.

Meanwhile, Elgol and Ella had taken off to go down to Croggan, being careful to avoid the fish farm, so as not to annoy the gulls following their agreement.

It didn't take them long to get to Croggan to look for the Buzzard in the tree, past the pier by the waterfall.

They found it straight away but immediately sensed that, yet again, something was wrong. Buzzards are very territorial and Elgol and Ella were expecting him to take to the skies to see them both off, but it didn't, which was very strange.

At more or less the same time, Elgol and Ella, and Olly and Pollyhannah, came to the same conclusion - all the birds that they had seen were fake and weren't real! They all tested out their assumption by approaching the birds and found they were right. They all headed back to their meeting place, well ahead of four o'clock, to tell Callum and each other what they had found.

Callum listened intently when his friends told him what they'd found and he felt happy that his suspicions were correct. Callum left for home to tell his Dad what he had found.

At first Ally didn't believe him as it sounded incredible. He couldn't understand how Callum could possibly have found this out. Callum pestered his Dad though until he gave in and, more to keep him quiet than because he thought it was possible, agreed to take him down the loch to investigate further.

They got down the loch to the heron who was still where he was reported with Olly and Pollyhannah looking on. Ally approached the heron expecting it to fly away but it didn't. He got closer and closer until he was within touching distance. Ally touched the heron and it was stone cold and was stuffed! Ally couldn't believe it. One by one, they found all the birds until they got to line 56 - the magpie and yes, this was not real either.

Ally couldn't believe that he'd missed the fact that they'd reported a magpie when they are so rare on Mull – as Mull wildlife warden this should have made him suspicious.

Ally knew what he had to do.

He went to "SAYSF Tours" to confront them about the deception. As soon as Ally's Land-rover pulled up outside, SAYSF Tours knew that the game was up.

They were very remorseful and sorry for what they'd done.

Mr 'SAYSF Tours' said, trying to explain, "we moved to Mull and needed to make a living. We could see that there are lots of wildlife tours already established and that we'd never be able to compete so we needed an edge."

In their previous life, Mr 'SAYSF Tours' had been a taxidermist and had amassed quite a collection of stuffed birds. This was now wildly frowned upon and unethical, so he had given it up to concentrate on living animals, putting his vast knowledge to good effect by helping to educate other people.

He said to Ally "That's when we hatched our plan to strategically place them around the island. This way we could guarantee sightings for the tourists and we would soon become the number one wildlife tour operator on Mull! The competition was the perfect way to establish our credibility.'

Ally said to them "You'll have to face the music and tomorrow I'm calling a meeting of all the tour operators at Laura's Coffee Shop when you will have to explain yourselves.' Ally then left them to think about what they had done.

When Ally got home he told Callum what had happened and Callum felt quite sad as he had heard how upset "SAYSF" were at having been found out, when all they really wanted to do was live on the Island.

The next day everyone gathered at the Coffee Shop but this time there were no bacon baguettes!

Time was marching on and there was no sign of "SAYSF Tours". They didn't turn up and Callum thought they must have gone into hiding.

Ally was just about to tell the assembled crowd what had happened when the 'SAYSF Tours' vehicle pulled up outside. They both got out and proceeded to confess to the waiting wildlife tour operators what they had done.

There were some angry people who felt that they had been fooled and that all of their integrity had been brought into question and disrepute.

Everyone said their piece and they were all very cross. The only person that hadn't made any comment was Douglas and what happened next took them all by surprise.

He said "We can't carry on like this. It comes to something and is desperately sad that people have to resort to cheating to make a living.' He then put forward a plan to try and keep everyone happy..........

Douglas said "Each of the tour operators needs to have an area on the island where you can conduct your own tours and you don't encroach on one another patches."

In the past, SAYSF ran an internet business. Douglas went on, "In future, we will establish a bird watching internet site on Mull run by SAYSF. All of the tour operators will contribute towards the running of it and keeping it up to date. All operators will share sightings of wildlife on the SAYSF website, so making it easier to spot things. In addition, Mrs SAYSF has been a baker, so in future all of us will buy cakes for our tours from her."

Duncan also proposed that 10% from all bookings should be donated to the Otter Salvation Fund. Finally, all the stuffed birds would be donated to the museum at Mull so that visitors could see close up the beautiful and magnificent markings on these birds.

They all agreed and accepted SAYSF's apology, which meant that they could all stay on the island and in future they all agreed that there wouldn't be any more driving confrontations.

No one ever found the magpie though, it had completely disappeared - Olly and Pollyhannah though, did have a friend staying with them in their holt!

After their adventures in stopping the nest robbers, and solving the bird sightings mystery, life settled back into some degree of normality and the lazy days of summer were drawing to a close. It had been a long hot summer and the only downside had been the dreaded midges. It seemed like every time Elgol and his friends got together the first topic of conversation was what the midges were like in much the same way that the tourists talked about the weather. Olly and Pollyhannah always found this highly amusing as for some reason they never seemed to be that bothered by them, or maybe, they soon would be!

Chapter Four - The Great Storm

The weather had been fine on Mull for many weeks and Elgol and his friends had enjoyed a wonderful time playing as well as having fun with the tourists by playing hide and seek with them.

One morning Callum got up early and was watching television whilst he was having his breakfast. He watched intensely as the weather forecast came on, as the previous day, a storm had been predicted. Normally he didn't bat an eyelid as they always seemed to get the weather wrong on Mull. If they predicted sun then it would rain, and if they forecast rain, then it would be torrential rain!

This particular morning though the weather forecast on the television had red warning signs all over Mull. Not only were they forecasting heavy rain, storms too, so much so that they were issuing warnings to tie things down, be prepared for flooding, and it was likely that the ferry crossings to the island would be severely disrupted.

Callum thought that he'd better warn his friends – Olly and Pollyhannah, Ella and Elgol, so he arranged to see them later that morning.

They all met up at their favourite spot.

The first thing on Callum's mind was the fact that when anyone wanted to call a meeting it was a bit hit and miss, and relied on his friends bumping into each other. Callum had an idea!

"Next to our favourite spot, why don't we build a small cairn of stones? We'll leave the top stone off though, and when anyone wants to call a meeting they could simply place the top stone on the cairn. This way they will know that a meeting was being called."

"What a great idea!" they all responded.

With that they decided that they ought to practise putting the stone on top.

Olly and Pollyhannah managed it after a couple of failed attempts. Elgol then tried, first swooping down to pick up the stone and then gliding in to gently place the stone on top of the Cairn – he soon mastered it and actually found it good fun. The others knew that he would pick it up quickly as he now had the reputation of being the best acrobatic flyer on Mull.

Ella was the next to try and, just like Elgol, picked it up quickly – the others could see that there was a bit of competition between them.

Olly then said, "This is great - we know that we are holding a meeting but what we don't know is when!"

Callum replied, "I wondered who would be the first to ask this - I've got the answer. Whoever calls the meeting, once you've placed the top stone on the cairn, you then place stones on the bridge, so if it's one o'clock then you put one stone on, two stones for 2 o'clock, and so on."

They all thought this was a good idea and promised to give it a go.

This had taken Callum a lot longer to sort than he had first thought and he'd nearly forgotten why he'd called the meeting in the first place!

Callum said, "Listen, I've been watching the television this morning and on the weather forecast they've issued a storm warning for Mull – they say it's going to be bad."

They all looked around at the bright sunshine without a cloud in the sky and Elgol said, "You're pulling our legs!"

They all chipped in and Callum was just thinking that he'd wished he'd kept quiet about the storm. Pollyhannah then said "Don't be so mean towards Callum!" They all then started laughing!

Olly explained "We know all about the storm that's coming. We don't have to rely on the television for the weather forecast, which is just as well, as we all know that they regularly get it wrong."

Olly added "Otters can tell what the weather is going to do from the tides, wind direction, where the moon is, where the fish swim, and the sun and the stones on the shore."

Callum was intrigued and asked, "How on earth can an otter tell what the weather is from the stones on the shore?"

and Olly replied, with a smile on his face "Well," spinning it out, "it's easy really, if the stones are wet……….. then it's raining!"

Once again they all burst out laughing - this time Callum joined in!

Elgol then said "Birds can also tell the weather days in advance by similar methods." Callum was starting to think that perhaps he ought to become a weather forecaster when he grew up provided his friends didn't feed him wrong information!

After the fun they'd had with Callum they all agreed that the weather was going to take a turn for the worse and that they were all fearful that it could cause them problems. They, each in turn, explained what they were going to do to protect themselves.

Elgol said "Mum and I are going to go fishing this afternoon and stock up with enough fish for a few days - then we're just going to stay in our nest until the storm blows itself out. Our nest is well built in the Tall Trees that have been around for over 100 years so we're confident that we will be fine."

Ella added, "That sounds like a good plan. I'll talk to Mum and Dad – I'm sure we'll be fine, it's not like we're not used to a bit of dampness!"

Olly and Pollyhannah said "We're going to do something similar. We are going fishing too. Eat as much as possible, and then take some additional fish home with us. Our normal home is just up the river from our meeting place but when we've had a lot of rain we have another holt further upstream which doesn't flood and we are planning on moving in there for a few days. It will need some clearing out though, as we've recently evicted a family of mink who have left it in a right mess!"

Callum then said "I'm going to be busy this afternoon as I am helping Dad get our animals under cover."

Callum was pleased that they all had a plan and it seemed they would all be ok.

Callum said, "If anyone has any problems at all please use our new signalling system to call for help."

With that they wished each other luck and went their separate ways to get ready for the Great Storm.

Elgol and Ella did as they had told their friends and between them they were pretty much prepared and ready for the onslaught ahead.

For Olly and Pollyhannah though, it was a different story....

They both got back to their holt and were getting packed up and ready for the move upstream when Pollyhannah said, "Olly, I'm not feeling great at all, my throat has seized up and I'm running a temperature."

Olly was quite worried, especially with the storm approaching and, after moving her to the safety of their new holt, he said, "You don't look very well at all. You stay in the warm and dry and I will go fishing by myself for provisions."

Pollyhannah objected but didn't have the energy to argue with Olly and, for once, Olly put his paw down and insisted that she stay at home. Pollyhannah knew that arguing any more was futile.

Olly said "It's not a problem for me to do two fishing trips. I will be back before you know it." With that, off he went and spent quite some time fishing around the pontoon.

He hadn't been fishing long when a strong familiar smell came from one of the fishing boats - a strong fishy smell.... he went to investigate.

Gingerly, he boarded the boat, pretty sure that there was no one on board, but he was still very wary. He smelt around the back of the boat and saw one of the hatches ajar. The smell seemed to be coming strongest from there. He pushed the hatch open with his nose and paws and was amazed at what he saw. The hold was overflowing with fish. He jumped down, ate a couple and then put the biggest one he could carry in his mouth and climbed out of the hatch, jumped off the back of the boat and then headed upstream back to the second holt to find Pollyhannah.

Pollyhannah was surprised to see Olly back so soon and was even more surprised to see the size of the fish that he'd brought her.

Olly didn't let on where he'd got it from, preferring to bask in the limelight of being the heroic fisherman and provider!

Olly then said "I'm off to get some more."

Pollyhannah tried to persuade him not to go, "Olly, the fish that you've caught will be more than sufficient to see us through a couple of days."

Once again, Olly insisted on going back arguing, "We know the storm is coming but we don't know quite how long it is going to last so we need to be prepared!"

Pollyhannah wasn't happy but reluctantly agreed and off Olly went.

Meanwhile, Callum was helping his Dad get the sheep in before the storm broke. As he did, he could see the dark clouds rolling down the valley and the skies getting darker and darker.

With that Callum started to become quite fearful and he hoped that his friends would be alright in the storm - he did think about sheltering them in one of his Dad's barns but it was now too late to contact them.

Night began to fall and as Elgol tucked himself tightly into his nest with his Mum, the first drops of rain fell. His Mum, Rona said, "It will be okay. I will look after you and I'll make sure no harm comes to you."

him. Elgol was not frightened for himself but had a similar feeling to Callum in hoping that his friends would be alright. With that he nestled down to try and get some sleep as best he could.

Back at the farm Callum was in bed, snug as a bug in a rug, but was finding it difficult to sleep as he could hear the wind howling amongst the tall trees behind him. He felt that it was going to be a long night, a very long night indeed.

Unbeknown to Callum, Pollyhannah, who was still not feeling very well, was now starting to get worried. Olly had been gone on his second fishing trip for many hours and there was neither sight nor sound of him. The rain had started and was getting heavier and heavier and as she looked out of her new holt she could gradually see the water level rising. This, coupled with the sound of the wind, made for uncomfortable listening and Pollyhannah was worried, "Where on earth can Olly be?"

Things were made worse for Pollyhannah because, since their parents had died, she had never been separated from Olly for more than a few hours and never overnight before and never during such a storm.

"Oh where on earth can he be?" Pollyhannah's thoughts were consumed by this question.

The next few hours did nothing to allay Pollyhannah's fears - the wind and rain got worse and worse. What was normally a gently flowing stream now became a gushing river whose banks could not contain the volume of water.

Pollyhannah could hear boulders being dragged along the riverbed, trees were crashing down in Tall Trees forest and it was then she spared a thought for Elgol and Ella. 'I hope they're alright.'

It may have been because Pollyhannah was ill but she felt very emotional and she started to cry as she felt so frightened and alone.

It was at this point that she thought something bad must have happened to Olly. She knew that he would never have left her to face this horrid night on her own and she started to fear the worst.

The minutes passed like hours for Pollyhannah as there was no let-up in the storm. The wind was relentless and in her short life she had never seen rain like it - she thought to herself, 'Will it ever end?'

The storm carried on relentlessly and, even with the breaking of dawn and a new day this didn't bring any respite as the rain just kept falling and the wind was wreaking havoc on their small island. Pollyhannah dreaded to think what the island would look like once the rain did stop. It carried on and on and Pollyhannah was now frantic. She just knew now that she had to do something as she feared for her brother and simply doing nothing wasn't an option.

The rain was torrential but Pollyhannah gathered all the energy that she had and decided to go and look for Olly herself.

She left the comparative safety of her holt and headed downstream or perhaps more appropriately down torrent to look for her brother. The current was really fierce and there was no way she could swim amongst the rapids. She had to make her way gingerly over rocks and boulders.

She got to what she thought was their old holt, but wasn't sure as everything looked completely different. She looked again and, yes, it was their old home where they had both been born and another tear entered her eye as her mind flashed back to her loving parents. This was no time to be sentimental though and she carried on downstream towards the loch.

Every step was a real effort, battling through the wind and rain. After what seemed an eternity, she reached their meeting place by the bridge. She was exhausted but she had the presence of mind to place a stone on top of the cairn to signal to her friends that she needed help (and she hoped that Olly would also see it). She was about to place stones on the bridge to indicate the time to meet but she collapsed, exhausted, under the bridge where she had taken shelter.

Back at the farm, Callum had woken early although, in truth, he hadn't slept a wink as he had been looking out of his window all night listening to the wind and rain battering the farm. Every minute that passed made him more fearful for his friends.

He had seen his father leave the comfort of the farmhouse earlier and had raced downstairs to go with him but his Dad stopped him saying "Stay here Callum. I'm only going to tie up one of the barn doors that's banging in the wind. I won't be long."

Callum, though, was worried about his friends and decided to go to their meeting place to check to see if they were ok. He put on his wet weather clothes, coat and wellies and headed out.

It didn't take him long to work out that his bicycle wasn't going to be a good idea this morning. The wind had dropped slightly and the rain was what his Dad would have referred to as "steady", even if most other people would have described it as a downpour!

He got to within sight of the bridge and saw that there was a stone on top of the Cairn and with that he quickened his pace and started running as he thought someone must be in trouble.

At the same time, Elgol had left their nest having been motionless for a long time and his wings were stiff and very wet. He took to the skies and what he saw was a scene of total devastation.

There were trees blown down everywhere, waterfalls flowing down the mountains in places that he'd not seen before and parts of the road alongside the loch had been washed away. At the campsite caravan awnings had blown down and were now amongst the trees and there were a couple of boats that had slipped their moorings and were lying on the shore at awkward angles.

Ella also took to the skies and looking across the loch the position was the same, with trees having blown down. There were tiles off roofs and she looked at the bridge in the village where the arch underneath was barely visible as the river was so high. Quite simply there was too much for her to take in and she thought to herself that this was perhaps one day when she wished her eyesight wasn't as good.

Elgol's mind quickly turned towards his friends and as he flew down towards the loch he could see Callum running to their meeting place. Elgol sensed that something was wrong, so very wrong, so he swooped into a dive to catch him up.

As he got closer he could see what Callum had seen, that there was a stone on top of the Cairn and he too started to worry.

They both reached the bridge at the same time. After some quick exchanges to check that they were both alright Callum said to Elgol "There's a stone on the cairn but there are no stones on the bridge!" They both concluded that something was wrong, but what, and where were Olly and Pollyhannah?

With that Callum was worried and looked under the bridge for any clues as to who had put a stone on top of the Cairn. He was shocked to see Pollyhannah unconscious, half in and half out of the water, but no sign of Olly. Callum pulled her out - she was very cold and he didn't know whether she was alive or not until he could see her breathing very faintly.

Callum said to Elgol "You must help, I will take Pollyhannah home with me. Dad will know what to do. Elgol, you go and find Olly."

Meanwhile Elgol was tasked with trying to find Olly. They both went their separate ways. Callum took off his coat and wrapped Pollyhannah in it gently to try and keep her warm and started carrying her home - he was quite surprised just how heavy she was. Pollyhannah seemed to come round slightly, calling out Olly's name before slipping back into unconsciousness. She was clearly worried about Olly.

Callum walked as quickly as he could back to the farm and at the same time Elgol flew off to try and find Olly. With the storm as fierce as it had been he knew that time was against him. Elgol soon realised, that Olly could be in a place inaccessible to a white-tailed eagle so he knew that he probably needed help.

His first port of call were the fish farm gulls as they had helped him out with the egg robbers previously. He flew down to the shore and met up with their leader - the very forbidding gull called Gus.

us was surprised to see Elgol as he had promised to give the fish farm a wide berth since the egg incident. Elgol explained that Olly was missing and could he help? Gus was initially a bit wary as otters were generally not friends of gulls, but when he realised it was Olly, he immediately offered to help as he had felt sorry for Olly and Pollyhannah when their parents had died, and he had regularly thrown fish scraps to them, gathered from one of the fishing trawlers.

Gus arranged the gulls into five squadrons of ten birds each and sent them all off in different directions with instructions to spread the word and to look for anything unusual, concentrating their search out to the sea and loch shores.

Gus said to them all, "Be back at the fish farm in an hour and if there's no luck then we will need to widen the search further."

Elgol then flew out across the loch, opposite the tall trees, where he saw some sheep running, having just been let out from the farm after the storm.

He thought he would go and ask them to keep an eye out for Olly. He flew down but before he could get close enough to talk to them they all scarpered in different directions as they'd been conditioned into running like the clappers from white-tailed eagles even though they were now far too big to be under any threat from them. 'Stupid animals' Elgol thought!

Elgol spent the rest of the morning asking for help from all his animal and bird friends, highland cattle,

gannets,

buzzards,

seals,

A kestrel,

And an osprey who had been blown off course on his way back to Spain - he had problems of his own but still promised to keep a beady eye out for Olly.

Elgol was quite exhausted now and couldn't think what else to do other than to keep circling the area.

Back at the farm, Callum had returned but his father wasn't there. Duncan, the gamekeeper from the local estate, had called by looking for help. A baby fawn had got caught in a gate and was stuck fast. The fawn's mother was going frantic and Duncan needed some help to free it. Ally had gone with Duncan to help and he left a note on the kitchen table to say where he was.

It was therefore down to Callum to look after Pollyhannah. He took Pollyhannah into the kitchen and made a bed of blankets in front of the Aga to keep her warm, Callum then rang their friend Graham from the Otter Salvation Fund in Tobermory to ask for help.

Luckily, he was in and Callum explained what had happened.

 Graham said, "Keep the otter warm and give her sips of water through a bottle. I'm then going to call Cameron the vet to see if he can pop out and see her."

Callum started nursing Pollyhannah as instructed and slowly Pollyhannah came round.

Callum's Dad and Duncan had arrived at where the fawn had got stuck. They were surprised to see the fawn just lying calmly, albeit firmly, stuck halfway through the gate.

The mother, who was watching from a safe distance, was far more agitated - helpless at not being able to do anything to save her baby. Duncan could see the predicament - clearly the fawn had got stuck and the more that it tried to push itself through the more stuck it got as its hind legs were a lot bigger than its front ones. If only it had reversed it would have been fine.

Ally grabbed the fawn's head and Duncan its back legs and they pushed the fawn back through the gate. The fawn let out this huge squeal, but they carried on and in no time the fawn was free.

The fawn must have been stuck for quite some time. Ally and Duncan guessed that it must have seen the storm out there.

As it walked slowly away, moving from side to side, it looked as if it were drunk but as the blood circulation improved she skipped away and looked none the worse for her ordeal.

They watched for several minutes and knew that it would be ok when they saw the fawn reunited with its mother.

They both felt very happy having done their good deed for the day; little did they know this wouldn't be their last!

Not far away, back at the fish farm, the squadrons of gulls were reporting back to Gus. They all had stories to tell of what they'd seen and the damage caused by the storm but none of them had seen the lost otter.

The osprey returned with one of the squadrons and he said that he hadn't seen anything but he had heard something a bit unusual. He described it "It was a funny noise like a mouse coming from a boat by the pontoons." Gus thought that the osprey was still confused but thought he'd mention it to Elgol when he returned.

As Duncan and Ally were heading back to the farm they drove past the pontoon. Duncan asked, "Can I stop quickly just to check on the new fishing boat there. The estate had only taken delivery of it last week and it's been quite a storm?"

Ally said "No problem, though it will cost you a few mackerel!"

Duncan readily agreed "Deal!"

Ally watched Duncan row out to the anchored boat. He watched Duncan get on the boat and check it over. He went to the back of the boat, bent down and, after a few seconds, Ally saw something quickly jump off the back of the boat, but he had no idea what it was. Duncan then got back in the rowing boat heading back to the shore.

Elgol circled back to the fish farm and shouted to Gus "Is there anything to report?"

Gus replied, "No, it's all quiet and there haven't been any sightings of Olly."

Elgol was just about to fly off to check with the seals when Gus shouted, "Hang about, there was one thing. The osprey reckoned he heard a noise like a mouse on one of the fishing boats at the pontoon, although I do think he's been hearing things!"

Elgol thanked him and set off to investigate - this was the best lead, in fact the only lead they'd had all day!

Duncan got back to the Land-rover and jumped in. Ally asked him "What was it that jumped into the water at the back of the boat?"

Duncan explained, "It was an otter, I was checking one of the hatches that we use to keep fish in and as I opened it this otter jumped out. I don't know who was frightened the most! The otter then jumped overboard and swam away as quickly as he could."

"I looked in the hatch and he must have been there a while as all the fish had gone - at least he hasn't gone hungry!"

As they headed back to the farm they saw a white-tailed eagle flying towards the pontoon. This was Elgol going to check on the strange noise that the osprey had heard. He circled overhead for what seemed ages, calling and listening for a response, but could hear nothing. Gus was right, the osprey must have made it up.

With that, he decided to go and find the seals on the other side of the island to see if they'd seen anything.

Back at the farm, Duncan and Ally rolled up just in time to see Cameron the vet turning down the road. They both wondered what he'd been doing at the farm. As they entered the kitchen it all became clear as they saw the otter in a bed by the Aga. Thankfully it appeared to be on the mend as it was picking on a small piece of mackerel. Ally said to Callum "What's that otter doing eating my tea!"

remarked that the otter was eating his tea! Duncan replied "Don't worry Ally, I'll get you some more."

Callum explained to his Dad and Duncan what had happened and how he'd found the half dead otter, how he'd carried it home, then called Graham for some advice who'd told him to call the vet.

Duncan listened intently and then said "Well that's a coincidence" and he told Callum what had happened to him on the fishing boat.

Both Callum and Pollyhannah's ears pricked up and both thought that this must be Olly. It just had to be as it would explain why he'd not gone home to Pollyhannah. It was the only explanation, or so they hoped!

When everyone had left, Callum said to Pollyhannah "That sounded really hopeful didn't it? Don't worry I'll go and find him, I am sure he will be fine." Pollyhannah pleaded with Callum to go with him but she was far too weak and Callum insisted that she stayed put.

At the pontoon Olly was now free from his ordeal. After leaving Pollyhannah at the holt to go and find some more fish on the fishing boat, he'd got on board and was in the hatch, sorting through the fish to find the largest one, when he heard the water lapping against the boat and some voices. He became frightened and buried himself under some fish.

After a while, it all went quiet again apart from the rain lashing down on the deck. The boat was rocking from side to side in the wind and Olly thought "I've had enough of this; I need to get back to Pollyhannah." He grabbed the largest mackerel he could find and pushed against the hatch. It didn't budge. He tried again, still no movement and again, and again, until he frantically kicked with all his might - quite simply, there was no way out unless someone opened the hatch from the outside. He could hear the rain lashing down and the boat was now really moving violently.

Quite bizarrely, the movement was making him feel quite seasick and he thought to himself that he must be the only otter in the world to feel seasick. Whilst he was frightened, what scared him even more was the thought of Pollyhannah back at the holt all on her own. She was poorly, and now she would be worried about where he was and he just hoped that she was alright and that she hadn't been foolish enough to try and go and look for him.

It was these thoughts that he tried to shut out of his mind as there wasn't a thing that he could do about them.

He then thought, "What can I do? There is absolutely no point in calling out until the storm subsides as no one would hear; maybe when it was over Elgol or someone would hear my cries."

He looked around for other ideas and all he could see were lots and lots of mackerel - there's only one thing for it he thought and began comfort eating his way through the fish in the hatch.

Time dragged on and on. The storm seemed to last an eternity and he had no idea how long he'd been locked up for but gradually the patter of the rain started to subside and the rocking of the boat got less and less. When it had calmed down he started shrieking a high frequency whine – this being his alarm call. Anyone hearing it would know that he was in trouble. What he hadn't reckoned on was being heard by a Spanish osprey whose animal translation left a lot to be desired!

He continued calling for hours and was about to give up when he heard the familiar sound of lapping water against the boat and he knew that someone was approaching. He heard the footsteps on the boat and hoped that whoever it was would open the hatch. If they did, he wasn't going to hang around and he was going to make a bolt for it and jump overboard as quickly as he could.

He heard the person checking around and he seemed to be going down the steps to get off the boat. Olly knew that he had to do something as he didn't know how much longer he could survive without water. He started to make a scratching noise as loud as he could. He sensed the footsteps stop on the ladder and then turn and jump back onto the deck. The person slowly opened the hatch and just as he said "Where on earth have all the fish gone!" Olly jumped out as if in one movement and, in the blink of an eye, had disappeared over the side of the boat.

Olly had made his escape and his priority now was to find Pollyhannah. He made his way past their meeting place, past their old holt that was totally flooded and completely underwater, and finally got back to their second holt.

He called to Pollyhannah but there was no reply. He went in and found the holt empty and he was now really worried that something terrible had happened to Pollyhannah. Where on earth could she be?

He went back to the meeting place, put a stone on the cairn and then went back to the loch to try and find Pollyhannah. She must have gone looking for him - if only he'd told her where he had caught the fish, he thought.

Callum got to the bridge and saw the cairn but he couldn't work out who had placed the stone on the cairn. He knew that Elgol and Ella were across the other side of the loch so it couldn't be them; Pollyhannah was back at the farm; and it wasn't himself so it had to be Olly. This was the only explanation.

Callum was excited about finding Olly and started shouting his name. Elgol was flying back and heard Callum shouting to him and wondered what the commotion was all about. Elgol then saw Olly swimming in and out of the kelp on the loch shore. He flew down and was so pleased to see him he shouted, "Where on earth have you been, Olly?"

Olly was also pleased to see Elgol and said "It's a long story - where's Pollyhannah, is she alright?"

"Yes," said Elgol, "She's fine, Callum's looking after her." They both then headed back to their meeting place.

Everyone recounted their stories about what had happened. All Olly was concerned about was getting Pollyhannah back home and Callum promised to get her to the holt just as soon as he could. By the time Callum got home you'll never guess where Pollyhannah was, playing in the laundry basket. I think that Ally had put two and two together and realised that this was the second time that this little otter had been playing in his kitchen!

Later that day, Callum and Ally put Pollyhannah in one of the dog travel cages and took her down to the loch by the pontoon. They opened the cage and Pollyhannah slipped away into the water. Ally swore that he saw her look back and give him a wink of thanks as she made her way back to her holt.

Waiting outside the holt was Olly. He was as pleased to see her, as she was him and they started playing and rolling around in the water, so relieved to be back together. Pollyhannah then said "What do you want for tea?"

Olly replied, "I don't mind really, provided it's not mackerel!"

Chapter Five The Treasure Hunt

It was some weeks after the great storm on Mull and the devastation was still around for all to see. Quite surprisingly, the storm had made national headlines and this had led to an influx of visitors, some of whom wanted to see the damage first hand and others who had come to help with the clean-up operation.

Life was getting back to normal for Elgol and his friends, then one day Elgol noticed that a meeting had been called as there was a stone on top of the cairn. He looked on the bridge and saw two stones on top. He knew this meant that they should meet up at 2 o'clock. Elgol wondered who had called the meeting and why, but, he'd make sure that he'd be there. Callum went by later that morning and saw the stone on the cairn but when he looked on the bridge he saw one stone so set his watch to return at one o'clock.

It turned 1 o'clock and Callum was waiting under the bridge. No one came he was starting to get a bit bored as there are only so many stones that you can throw into the river to pass the time. Luckily he'd brought his binoculars with him so spent the time watching a couple of wading birds foraging amongst the kelp.

Time moved on and he sensed Elgol flying in behind him with a swoosh of his wings – Callum looked at his watch and said "Hello Elgol, what time do you call this - the meeting was called for one o'clock?"

Elgol argued "No, the meeting was called for 2 o'clock as there were two stones on the bridge when I flew past earlier today." Callum said, with a smile on his face "You'd better get your eyes tested then as there's only one stone there now!"

They spent a little time pondering what had happened to the stone but more interestingly, why Olly and Pollyhannah had called the meeting and where on earth were they?

They talked about the storm and how quiet it was on the loch now that the road had been closed due to a rock-slide. They both agreed that they were in no rush to have the road re-opened, even if it did mean a 35-mile diversion for traffic!

After what seemed a long time, they heard a splish-splash and they both said in unison "Here they are, at last!"

"What do you mean?" Olly replied "We're bang on time - 3 o'clock!"

Callum said to Olly and Pollyhannah, "Look on the bridge" and there, true enough, was only the one stone.

They then began debating as to what had happened as they were all adamant as to what they'd seen. They couldn't understand who had moved the stones. Surely no one had been watching them, discovered what they were doing and had moved the stones to confuse them.

They were all thinking who it might be - Callum thought it might be cheeky Rhys from school, Elgol thought it might be the gulls and Olly and Pollyhannah thought it might be.... when all of a sudden there was an almighty splash and they all got soaked as the remaining stone on the bridge fell into the stream.

"What the blazes is going on?" Elgol shouted and they all looked up to see a highland cow scratching its back on the wall of the bridge.

Pretty quickly, they all put two and two together and realised that this is how the time got changed - the highland cow had inadvertently pushed the stones off the bridge. They were all quite relieved, if a little wet, that no one had infiltrated their group of friends.

Now that little mystery had been sorted, Elgol asked Olly and Pollyhannah "What did you want to meet for?"

Olly said "We've got a cousin otter in Tobermory called Shadow and he's quite a celebrity. Shadow is going on his holidays across the Sound of Mull to Ardnamurchan where there's a rock festival being held at Knoydart. People come from far and wide to listen to the music."

Olly added, "Shadow has gone to this concert for many years and that's how he got his name - every time a Shadows' song could be heard, out he'd pop to charm the crowds - the tourists in Tobermory soon became wise to this and so called the otter 'Shadow' with many people then remarking that the Shadows were playing in Tobermory harbour!"

Elgol said, "All very interesting, I'm sure but I'm getting hungry. What's this got to do with us?"

Olly said "Well not much really, but Pollyhannah and I have been invited to go and stay with Shadow's Mum and Dad in Tobermory and it could be quite fun. Apparently, you get as much food as you can eat, you get your photograph taken and you could also appear on the internet on YouTube, whatever that is! This means that we're not going to be about for two weeks but we'll miss you all."

Now life was never the same when one of the group was missing and it was bad enough when Callum had to go to school. The thought of them not meeting up for two whole weeks didn't go down well with any of them.

They started thinking about how they could keep in touch, but apart from a few silly suggestions, no one could think of anything.

Elgol then piped up. "I've got it! We'll all come with you!"

Callum said, "What? We can't all go with Olly and Pollyhannah to Tobermory, can we?"

Elgol then said, "Yes we can. You've also got a cousin, Faye, who lives in the old lighthouse at Tobermory. Why don't you ask to stay with her?"

Elgol said "Olly and Pollyhannah will be taken care of and I will go and stay with my Auntie and Uncle at Glengorm Castle. They've got a monster of a nest and they've always said that I'd be welcome to stay any time. Glengorm is only a stone's throw away from Tobermory and I've always fancied being Laird of the Castle even if only for two weeks! You will, though, all have to call me Lord, he added!"

They all thought this was a magnificent idea, apart from calling Elgol, Lord!

They all left to put their plans into action. What an adventure they'd have! They all agreed to meet at the same time tomorrow and then started arguing as to what is the same time tomorrow - one, two or three o'clock! They settled on two o'clock and the highland cow was definitely not invited.

One by one, they sorted out their holiday plans and spoke to everyone that they needed to, to get approval. They met the following day and were all excited about the prospect of going to Tobermory on holiday.

Olly and Pollyhannah were going on the Friday as Shadow had agreed to show them the ropes and give them the guided tour of Tobermory Harbour. Elgol and Callum would be going on the Saturday.

Olly asked "Where are we going to meet up on Saturday?"

Elgol said "I know the ideal place - several hundred yards from the old lighthouse there's a tidal bell that sounds at high tide. We can all meet there."

They all agreed and went off to pack their bags. They couldn't wait until the weekend.

It was quite a swim for Olly and Pollyhannah, but it didn't take them long and they arrived in Tobermory Harbour early on the Friday morning. They soon met up with Shadow using the sixth sense that otters have.

"Well, hello" he greeted them, "Welcome to the St Tropez of Mull, this is where all the action and excitement happens! Let me show you around."

Shadow took them around the harbour and told them who to look out for and where they could get fed. His favourite spot was on the harbour wall by the cross, or perhaps more accurately the famous 'Chirpy Cheryl's Chip Shop.' Although, he'd never ever met Chirpy Cheryl!

Linda and Karen had been serving fish and chips there for many years and Trip Advisor rated them amongst the best fish and chips in Scotland. When asked their secret, they responded that the reason that they were so good was that they tasted every single batch to check the quality - although this did have some consequences!

What was even better was that Linda and Karen were Shadow's best friends and they always kept some fish back so that he too "checked every batch" and he could vouch for their quality even if he hadn't mastered Trip Advisor!

Shadow told Olly and Pollyhannah about the Otter Salvation group and, if they ever needed help, where to go to find Graham - a name familiar to Pollyhannah as he had helped her when she fell ill during the Great Storm on Mull last year.

Shadow then said "I must tell you about Daisy." "Who's Daisy?" they both asked.

Shadow said, "Daisy's the Tobermory dog and the nicest dog you'll ever meet, and she's my best friend. In the summer we've even been known to cuddle up asleep on the rocks below the harbour wall together – Daisy and her Shadow."

They then went swimming around the harbour in and out of the boats and out into the mouth of the harbour.

"I need to tell you about the underwater cavern." said Shadow adding, "There's a giant crab that protects the cavern and you shouldn't go anywhere near it." Olly and Pollyhannah thought that Shadow was pulling their legs but they could tell by the tone of his voice that he was deadly serious.

Pollyhannah asked "What's the crab protecting?"

Shadow replied, "You don't want to know." This made them both even more intrigued but they could tell that Shadow was not for sharing so they decided to drop it - for now in any event!

They went back to the harbour and Shadow said "See you in two week's folks and have a great time. Look after Daisy and don't eat too many chips!"

"Have fun!" Olly and Pollyhannah replied and with that Shadow started his swim across the Sound of Mull.

Olly and Pollyhannah had had a busy day so decided to have an early night as they suspected the next couple of weeks were going to be busy - little did they know how busy!

Callum arrived in Tobermory on Saturday morning. His Dad had dropped him off at the old lighthouse where Aunty Betty and Uncle Tom were waiting by the front door with their daughter Faye. Faye was a couple of years younger than Callum and she always tagged along with him. This could be a problem he thought, especially when meeting Elgol, Olly and Pollyhannah.

Callum unpacked and then went down to the shore to explore and to find the tidal bell. He wanted to see if his friends had made it safely to Tobermory.

Elgol had also arrived on Saturday morning; he'd gone fishing on Loch Frisa on the way for breakfast and then flown on to Glengorm Castle. The nest was in trees overlooking the castle with views out over the ocean, "What a fantastic outlook!" Elgol thought.

His Aunty and Uncle were waiting for him and told him to make himself at home. They were both getting on a bit so he could foresee being left very much to his own devices, which suited him down to the ground. When he felt that he had exchanged enough pleasantries and that flying off would not be seen to be rude he told them he was off to explore, and flew off to Tobermory. On the way he passed over Mull Cheese and Tobermory distillery - he knew which smell he liked best!

Elgol got to the outskirts of Tobermory and heard a bell sounding. It was not high tide, so he knew it must be one of his friends. He flew towards the lighthouse; Olly and Pollyhannah also heard the bell and they too headed towards the lighthouse. They all arrived within minutes of one another and they were all so pleased to see each other. They shared stories of their journeys and what their holiday homes were like. Unbeknown to them, whilst they were chatting away, they were being watched by someone on the shore.

They started talking about what they were going to do on their holidays. Callum said "I'm so excited, Uncle Tom has told me I can borrow his canoe provided that I don't go out of the harbour and that I always wear my lifejacket." Callum, of course, readily agreed and thought this would be a great way to spend some time with his otter friends.

Elgol said "One day I'm planning to fly over to Lunga as it isn't far and the coast line is impressive."

Olly piped up and said "Isn't that where Ella has gone for her holidays?"

"Oh, is it?" said Elgol. Callum was sure that he was blushing!

Pollyhannah then said jokingly "Well, if anyone's interested I am going searching for buried treasure." They all laughed at her.

Callum said "The only buried treasure you'll find will be a couple of empty cola cans!"

Whilst they were discussing their plans, Olly told them what Shadow had said about the underground cavern and the giant crab. Elgol thought this was very fishy! They had a good laugh and each went their separate ways agreeing to meet up again tomorrow - Olly and Pollyhannah shot off quickly as they had an important meeting with a certain fish and chip shop. As they departed, the onlooker waited a few moments and then also slipped away undetected.

The next day, Olly and Pollyhannah were up early and went exploring the harbour. They had so much fun swimming in and out of the boats and playing hide and seek with holiday makers. They could see why Shadow was treated like a pop star and how he'd got his name! Pollyhannah said that she wanted to explore the cavern but Olly wouldn't let her. She thought that he was a little frightened in truth.

Pollyhannah though, pestered and pestered him, as only she knew how, until he gave in and off they both went. They got close to the underground cavern and were mooching amongst the kelp which was swaying with the current when all of a sudden "whoosh!"

There was a big flash with a bright light in what seemed to them like an explosion and the sand became disturbed from the seabed so that they couldn't see through the water. They then heard a voice shout "go away......!" Olly and Pollyhannah didn't stay around long enough to listen anymore and off they shot as fast as they could.

Once they were a safe distance away they hopped on board an empty rowing boat moored up in the harbour and they both let out a sigh of relief.

Olly then said, "That was close!"

Pollyhannah said "I actually think that the giant crab is lonely and just wanted someone to talk to."

Olly said "I think that you are probably right but I won't be talking to him again anytime soon."

Pollyhannah then asked Olly, "What did you make of the flash?" He replied "I don't know it was like a golden blur but, no matter what it was, I'm not about to go back to find out!"

Olly could tell that Pollyhannah wasn't going to let this drop and that this wasn't going to be the end of the matter.

Callum also got up early and he helped his Uncle Tom in the garden. They dug out a new vegetable patch; it was hard work but very rewarding. After lunch he decided to go and look for his friends and was about to go down to the tidal bell when Faye asked "Where are you going?"

Callum responded "I'm going for a walk."

Faye asked him "Can I come with you to play with your friends as well?"

Callum stepped back in surprise, "What friends?" he said.

"You know, the animals," Faye replied. Callum asked "How do you know about them?"

She said "I followed you yesterday and saw you at the tidal bell."

Callum didn't know what to do - his initial reaction was to deny it and to tell her she couldn't come with him, but she would only persevere and she could easily tell her friends, so he decided to confide in her. "Okay," he said "You can come with me but you must promise to keep this a secret." She agreed and off they went.

Meanwhile, Elgol had been up early and had flown to Lunga where, coincidentally, he'd met up with Ella. They'd spent a lovely morning flying around together and then fishing. They both decided to fly back to Tobermory. On the way, they flew over a strange boat heading to the harbour. It had a big crane on the back and a strange tank-like object which they had never seen before. They agreed that they would tell Callum about it when they met up.

When they all reached the bell, Olly explained what had happened at the underground cavern and they were all in agreement that they wanted to know more, as none of them could explain the golden flash. Elgol and Ella told them about the boat that they'd passed and Olly and Pollyhannah said that they'd keep an eye on it, and report back anything suspicious. Faye sat there with a smile on her face and Callum asked her, "Why are you smiling?"

Faye said "I know what the boat is."

Elgol asked her "How do you know about the boat?"

She said "It was in last week's Tobermory Times. There's a salvage operation in the harbour starting this week, so that must be what the boat is doing heading for Tobermory."

Callum asked Faye "What are they salvaging?" But she didn't know.

Callum said "I'll read the article and report back - in the meantime please all of you keep your eyes and ears open!"

When Callum and Faye got back they looked for last week's Tobermory Times. Faye found it in the wood basket where they kept old newspapers to light fires with and she fished it out and gave it to Callum.

It seemed that a boat had sunk in the harbour many years ago and that there was some treasure on board - the salvage boat was heading to Tobermory to look for it. Callum wanted to know more. Faye said that she had done a project on it at school during her history lessons and the best place to find out more was to visit the Tobermory Museum. They took the newspaper with them and they headed into town.

They got to the museum and started talking to the curator about the sunken boat. He sat them down and proceeded to tell them the whole story.

"The ship was called La Forencia and was part of the Spanish Armada that had set sail to attack England in 1650. Most of the ships were sunk by the English navy but several fled to the far corners of the world. La Forencia had headed north to try and escape and had entered Tobermory Harbour just as a fierce storm was brewing (pretty much like the Great Storm of a few weeks ago). The ship was apparently carrying a load of gold bullion that was being used to finance the invasion. The storm got worse and worse, so much so that La Forencia sank without trace in Tobermory Harbour and no one had ever found any trace despite a lot of people looking over the years."

Callum and Faye sat mesmerised and were hanging on every word - you could have heard a pin drop.

Callum asked "Why has no one ever found anything - the harbour is quite small?"

The curator explained "This happened so long ago and would have been covered by thousands of tonnes of sand and silt. The harbour is in waters owned by the Duke of Argyle and over the years he's mounted several salvage operations and they have all been unsuccessful."

Callum then remembered the Tobermory Times and asked about the article.

The curator said, "The Duke had been approached by a rich American whose ancestors came from the Isle of Mull and he's offered to fund another salvage operation. Apparently he's made his money out of shipping. The Duke has agreed and the boat with a submarine on it is currently heading to Tobermory."

They both thanked the curator for his help and started heading back to the lighthouse for tea. By this time, the whole of Tobermory was awash with people. They hadn't seen so many people and couldn't understand why the place was so busy.

Since the newspaper article, the salvage operation had made the national headlines and had even been reported on the BBC. This had captured a lot of people's imaginations and many people had headed to Mull, and Tobermory, in particular, to see first-hand the salvage operation - there was a sense that something special was happening.

They got back home and asked Uncle Tom about the story of La Forencia. He said, "I've heard of the stories over the years but they're just stories made up to keep visitors intrigued, very much along the lines of the Loch Ness Monster!" He then added "If they find anything I'll swim across the Sound of Mull in my underpants!"

All of Callum's friends met up later that evening desperate to learn what Callum and Faye had found out. They told them everything. They were all very excited about the adventure that was about to begin.

Olly said "In the morning we'll ask around the harbour to see what we can find out."

They all agreed that they'd meet up again tomorrow.

Olly and Pollyhannah spoke to some seals and whilst they weren't particularly helpful they said to ask the giant crab. They also asked some eels and got the same response. When they got the same message from a dolphin they didn't have much choice other than to approach the giant crab.

They both plucked up courage and headed for the underground cavern to confront the crab - they both thought that if the worse came to the worse their speed and agility would save them.

They approached cautiously whispering "Crab, crab can we talk?"

At first there was nothing, then the silt began to stir and rather than the explosion that occurred last time, the crab gently emerged from the sea bed. "Oh it's you two again. I'm sorry I scared you last time but you frightened me" said the crab.

"Frightened you!" Olly said "you scared the living daylights out of us, we thought we were goners."

"Oops" said the crab, "I didn't mean to."

Olly then explained about the salvage operation and La Forencia. The crab didn't seem in the least bit surprised but, at the same time, looked very worried. "You'd better sit down, whilst I tell you the story" he said.

"It was true about La Forencia sinking in the harbour and yes, there was treasure on board. All the sea creatures over the years have agreed and promised that they would protect the harbour - their home - and not let anyone find the ship and the treasure. If it was to be found Tobermory Harbour would never be the same again. This promise had been passed down from generation to generation and it's now my turn to protect the treasure."

Olly said "But there's been lots of salvage operations in the past and none have found the ship so, don't worry, they won't find it now."

The crab said "Yes that's right, over the year's silt has buried the treasure and it is now so deep that the only way to find it is by the underground cavern and that was why I was protecting the entrance."

Pollyhannah interrupted saying "Surely the ship is safe then?"

The crab said, "It was and has been for many years but the Great Storm a few weeks ago must have been as ferocious as the one that sank the La Forencia all those years ago. The storm has shaken up the whole of the seabed and rather than being buried under metres of silt it is now just below the surface and actually some of the gold coins are now on the sea bed."

Pollyhannah said "That must have been what I saw when you scared us last time, the gold flash must have been a gold coin!"

The crab agreed. "All this is very well, but what are we going to do?" He was very worried.

Olly said to him, trying to reassure him "Don't worry, I'll report back to my friends and we'll come up with a plan."

The crab felt relieved but said "You need to act quickly as the treasure could be found any day."

They all knew what it was like to have time against them.

The following day Olly and Pollyhannah called a meeting and proceeded to tell their friends all about their encounter with the Giant Crab. They all agreed that they needed to help the crab to protect the ship - Tobermory Harbour was such a beautiful place and if the ship was found it could be turned into Las Vegas. They couldn't let this happen. They needed a plan and quickly!

Callum gave everyone their jobs to do.

He said, "Elgol and Ella, this is an emergency! Will you both fly over to Ardnamurchan to try and find Shadow? We need his help. He will know what to do."

"Olly and Pollyhannah, you will need to keep an eye on the boat and the tank on the back - this is actually a submarine and will be used in the salvage operation."

"Faye and I will go down to the harbour to see what we can find out and see what they are planning; we will all meet back here later." With that, off they went.

Elgol and Ella flew over the Sound of Mull and, from high in the sky, could see how big a place Ardnamurchan was - this was going to be like looking for a needle in a hay-stack! They decided to split up and each take one end of the peninsula and meet in the middle.

Olly and Pollyhannah went back to the harbour and decided to call at the chip shop on the way as they were ravenous. When they got there they'd never seen anything like it. Clearly, the crowds of people were hungry and the queue stretched past the Co-op, past the Post Office and beyond the ice-cream shop.

Linda and Karen though, maintained their stance on quality by checking every batch - Olly heard Karen say "We'd best give Slimming World a miss this week!" Olly and Pollyhannah gave up on the chip shop and headed across the harbour to report back to the crab to try and reassure him.

Callum and Faye went down to the boatyard and started asking questions. They found out that they were planning on starting the search on Monday. Initially they would start by the shore and then gradually they would increase the radius every day - apparently they'd allocated two weeks for the search as the submarine was needed for an exploration chasing sharks in the Atlantic!

Callum managed to meet the Captain and started talking to him about the salvage operation. He could tell that the man was warming to him and talked quite freely and even offered to help him with his studies.

Callum then asked the Captain, "How will the submarine search for the treasure?"

The Captain replied, "On the front of the submarine are a series of metal detectors that are so sensitive that they can detect metal through 10 metres of silt. If the treasure's there then we'll find it!"

This made Callum very worried.

On the way back from the harbour Faye said,

"My dad's got a metal detector - maybe it's worth speaking to him to find out more?" They both then went back to the lighthouse to find Uncle Tom.

Uncle Tom was there painting the fences. He thought something was wrong when they both offered to help him! They got chatting about the metal detector and after they had finished he agreed to take them down to the seashore to try it out.

They got to the shore and Callum had a go. It wasn't long before it beeped - he was so excited about his find until he realised it was an old baked bean tin! Faye then had a go and after a while another beep - again she was excited but this time it was some cheese sandwiches that someone must have thrown into the sea.

Faye was confused and asked her dad, "How can cheese set off a metal detector?"

Her dad explained "Sometimes food can throw off electro-magnetic currents that confuse metal detectors." This gave them both an idea and whilst they were having fun they knew they had some work to do!

Elgol and Ella were working hard to find Shadow and it was the sound of music that attracted them to the seashore - they realised that this was their best chance of finding him. They flew down to the shore and there they saw him dancing in and out of the kelp with a Shadows track appropriately pounding out across the water from the Rock Festival.

Ella approached Shadow trying not to scare him. She explained about the salvage operation - he was clearly shaken and said, "I need to get back to Mull as soon as possible."

Elgol said "We'll meet you back at the tidal bell just as soon you can get there."

It was high tide and the bell started chiming. Within minutes, everyone arrived on the shore including Faye, Shadow and even the giant crab, who had managed to get an octopus family to keep an eye on the cavern. They were all worried about the galleon being found, but none more so than the Giant Crab who was feeling the pressure of having the responsibility of keeping the treasure safe.

Callum said "We need to come up with a plan to make sure that the galleon remains undiscovered for another 400 years!"

Faye had found out how the salvage operation was going to operate and she thought that it would only take a few days for the submarine to reach the galleon; this didn't give them much time. They then all contributed ideas as to how they could thwart the salvage operation.

Callum summarised their discussion "Right, our mission is to – 'Sabotage, Decoy, Confuse and Give Up.' That's them give up not us Pollyhannah!"

The 'SDCGU Mission' was born.

They all had their jobs and knew what to do – nobody quite knew what tomorrow would bring but they all knew they would need to be alert and needed a goodnight's sleep.

The next day, Faye and Callum got up and made their way down to the harbour. They started by going into every shop on the high street asking for empty cans. They told everyone that it was for a project they were doing to help protect the environment! When people heard this they readily agreed to help.

After scouring the high street Faye rang round her school friends and they all agreed to help, although a lot asked more questions than the shopkeepers! In the afternoon they tackled the bars, cafés, hotels and restaurants. Once they had spoken to everyone they went back later in the afternoon to collect their cans.

Meanwhile, Elgol and Ella had flown back to the fish farm where they'd met up with Gus and his gang. As usual, Gus wasn't very pleased to see them but was curious to find out what they wanted this time. Whatever it was it was usually fun and exciting!

Elgol and Ella explained 'We need help in annoying a boat that's looking for the galleon in Tobermory harbour.'

Gus knew of the story but was not very forth-coming and asked "Ok, but what's in it for us?"

Elgol said, "There's loads of visitors in Tobermory."

Before he could finish Gus interrupted, "We're in!" It hadn't taken Gus long to work out that this meant they needed feeding, which in turn meant eating fish and chips (Gus was aware of the chip shop's reputation) which meant easy pickings for hungry gulls!

With that the gulls headed off towards Tobermory - not quite like the Red Arrows but more like a swarm of bees heading towards a honey-pot.

Shadow had been swimming around the harbour and had kept quite close to the salvage boat trying to hear what was going on. He was trying to keep tabs on them and to see what their plan for the day ahead was. He learnt that they were going to start nearest to the shore and then work out in a semi-circular radius. He also learnt that time was against them as the submarine was needed across the other side of the world - if only they could slow them down sufficiently, they might just give up, he thought and hoped!

Shadow met up later with Olly and Pollyhannah who were by the giant crab protecting the cavern and talking about their decoy plan. The salvage boat had created a lot of interest around Tobermory, not just from interested onlookers, but also from divers wanting to get rich quickly. To a diver this was the ultimate adventure. The divers tended to search a bit further afield out into the Sound of Mull, as the salvage boat had an exclusive arrangement to search in the harbour. Olly and Pollyhannah's plan was for Elgol to take one of the gold coins and drop it a good way out. If it was then discovered by a diver it would be a long way from the real treasure and would throw off a false trail.

At high tide they all met up to report back on their day's activities.

Elgol said, "Gus and his friends are now in the harbour having a ball making themselves a nuisance around the salvage boat."

This had really confused the people on the boat as the gulls only seemed to be targeting their boat. The gulls had found it quite amusing as the people on the boat had been trying to work out why. They'd each changed their jumpers as they thought it might be the colour; they'd hidden any sign of food; they put up flags; they'd pulled down flags - no matter what they'd tried, the gulls just kept coming back!

Now the gulls had also been making a nuisance of themselves by the chip shop and it was quite an amusing sight to see people with umbrellas up on a bright sunny day whilst trying to eat their fish and chips! So far this plan was working!

Faye then said "We've collected loads of empty cans and we're in the process of flattening them. We'll then need to take them out to the cavern early tomorrow morning so that Shadow, Olly, Pollyhannah and the giant crab can set about burying them by the cavern. The idea being that the metal detectors on the boat would spot something on their screens which would lead them to investigate they would realise they were just tin cans and then move on somewhere else!" Or at least that's what they hoped would happen.

The next day, Faye and Callum were up early, had their breakfast and then loaded up the canoe with tin cans. They set off from the lighthouse towards the underground cavern where Shadow, Olly, and Pollyhannah were already waiting. Faye and Callum started passing the flattened cans to Olly, Pollyhannah and Shadow. In turn, they created a layer of cans buried in the silt several metres above the buried treasure. The recent storm had really exposed the galleon, as previously, this would have been a lot deeper. After about an hour, Faye and Callum returned to get more cans. They managed to do one more trip before they could see the salvage boat getting closer on one of its sweeps of the harbour so had to call it a day before they raised suspicion.

The next day, it was a beautiful morning and, as the salvage operation got under way, it was a hive of activity as a whole host of divers also took to the water - Shadow had never seen so many people!

Olly, Pollyhannah and Shadow decided to have some fun with the visitors. Now, Shadow had become quite a celebrity in Tobermory and there was even a book written about him which added to his fame. Already visitors had spotted him and he took great delight in posing for photographs. Shadow told Pollyhannah and Olly to strategically place themselves at different places around Tobermory. Olly by the lifeboat and Pollyhannah by the harbour - let the game commence!

Shadow then popped out onto the harbour steps by the chip shop and was playing with the fishing rope on the harbour wall. It didn't take long for a little girl to spot him, and she immediately shouted, "Look there's Shadow, Mummy!"

No sooner had the words left her lips, than a hoard of photographers ran towards him; if he didn't know differently he would have been quite frightened.

After a few minutes he slipped quietly into the water out of sight. Following their pre-arranged signal, Olly popped out of the water and climbed up the anchor chain onto the back of the lifeboat where he started eating a crab he'd just caught (not the giant crab!). Again, an eagle-eyed little boy shouted to his daddy "there's Shadow!" All the people and photographers ran from the harbour wall like a stampede and headed for the lifeboat. There was so much excitement that even people in the queue for the chip shop abandoned their places to go and see Shadow.

After a couple of minutes Olly slipped down the anchor chain and back into the water out of sight. A few minutes later Pollyhannah popped out of the water the other side of Tobermory and this time proceeded to run up and down the pontoon. The people on the high street could see the commotion and ran to catch a glimpse of what they thought was Shadow. Just as they arrived, Pollyhannah slipped back into the water. Now that they'd all completed a turn at being Shadow they started the whole sequence over again – oh, how they smiled at the visitors running around like ants – it made such a change from hiding from tourists they thought!

This little exercise took up most of the day but at the same time they always had one eye on the salvage boat and submarine. Elgol and Ella were also keeping a watching eye, for now they weren't close, but it was only a matter of time and they needed to do more work with the cans.

The following day was more or less a repeat of the previous day, laying down cans first thing and then confusing the tourists - this was going fine until one bright spark noticed that Shadow had a cut over his eye caused by a fierce fight with a crab. The tourists then realised that there was more than one otter in Tobermory harbour!

By now, there was a real sense of excitement building in the town as everyone had become hooked on the idea of finding buried treasure on Mull. The general store was doing a roaring trade in pirate costumes and toy parrots; the pub had run out of rum and even the chip shop was cashing in by selling Long John Silver burgers!

The next day the sense of excitement came to a head when word had got round that the submarine had found something in the harbour. A part of the harbour was cordoned off where boats were not allowed to go and there was frantic activity on board the salvage boat, with boats going backwards and forwards to the shore. Faye and Callum looked on in some surprise as the area where they were looking was a long way from the galleon. After about an hour the excitement died down as it turned out that the metal detectors had picked up several truckles of cheese! They had been destined for the mainland from the local cheese factory but had been lost overboard in the recent storm - apparently they'd played havoc with the metal detectors. Faye thought she knew what that was like!

The search continued over the coming days with the submarine getting closer and closer to the gold. They were all getting worried and wondered what would happen if the tin cans didn't work.

Elgol then said "Right, now we need a decoy?"

Callum replied "What do you mean?"

Elgol said "What if we take a few of the gold coins and drop them in the ocean out at sea so that if found they would then focus their attention on looking for the gold in the wrong place."

Olly said, "That's our idea! When we mentioned it earlier you all dismissed it as being silly."

They all discussed the idea. There was a chance that if any gold was found it could work against them as it would prove that there was something worth searching for...... would it be found in any event? Dropping a coin in the ocean would be like looking for a needle in a haystack. On balance, they agreed that they had to do something, so Shadow would go and get some coins later that evening and Elgol and Ella would do the rest.

They all said goodnight and wished each other luck - tomorrow was the day when the submarine would be right over the treasure.

That day came all too soon and everyone was focused on the salvage boat. Around mid-day, a bell sounded on the boat and they knew that this signalled a find in the harbour, based on their experience from a few days ago.

They all became very worried as they faced the nail biting wait, wondering whether their plan would succeed. The weight of over 400 years was a huge responsibility to bear on their young shoulders and they just hoped that their plan would work.

The next ninety minutes was the longest of their lives as the submarine worked below the surface. The giant crab, quite rightly, had run off, or run off as best he could! All the otters, though, were keeping a close eye on the situation. They saw the submarine unearth the flattened cans - they even surprised themselves as to how many they found. Word soon got back to shore that it was another false alarm and Callum and his friends all breathed a huge sigh of relief. All they had to do now was hope that the submarine didn't continue its search in the area as it would surely find the treasure if it did, now that the cans had been removed.

Fortunately, the submarine moved on and continued its fruitless search elsewhere and the day came to a close. Callum and his friends got together to congratulate themselves at the tidal bell and everyone breathed a huge sigh, or they did until Shadow said "What about the gold coins that were dropped in the ocean?"

Elgol said "What about them?"

Shadow replied "If they were to be found then the focus would be back on trying to find the galleon again and we won't hear the last of this."

They all agreed that the coins had to be found - they couldn't leave it to chance for a diver to find. They asked Elgol where he'd dropped them, at which point a shiver went through his wings

"Well I don't really know, I just sort of dropped them" Elgol said.

It was no good - they had to be found.

Early the next day, they split up - Elgol went with Shadow and Ella went with Olly and Pollyhannah into the vicinities where Elgol thought he'd dropped the coins. Shadow went swimming along the seabed and Elgol flew over-head. Fortunately it was a lovely day and he was using his exceptional eyesight to try and pick out the coins.

Ella did similarly in another location. It was painstaking work and after many hours they were both on the verge of giving in when, within minutes of one another, they both had success and found some coins. However, there was one still missing and, despite everyone focussing on the area where Elgol thought he'd dropped the coin, it proved to be elusive. They all agreed that if they couldn't find it then chances were a diver wouldn't, so they would have to leave it to chance.

The following day they watched the submarine being packed away on the boat and leave the harbour on its way to America to do its study of sharks. Olly and Pollyhannah were so pleased that they didn't have to contend with killer sharks on Mull. Everyone was all smiles as they had managed to thwart the salvage operation - for now at least!

Faye and Callum went back home for tea and Uncle Tom asked them whether they would like to go down to the sea shore afterwards to look for treasure. They didn't have the heart to tell him that they had done enough treasure hunting to last them a lifetime, so they readily agreed.

On the way he asked them what had happened to the cans that they'd been collecting and didn't seem too surprised when they couldn't come up with a feasible explanation. He gave them a wry smile and then got out his metal detector. Within ten minutes the bleeper went berserk! He got out his little spade and started digging and you'll never know what he found - a Spanish gold coin.

He took one look and then gave it to Faye and said "You'd better put this back with the rest" and with that he winked and turned to head for home.

She replied "How are you fixed for swimming across the Sound of Mull, Dad, I'll hold your clothes?!"

Chapter Six   The Great Mull Air Mystery

At school, Callum had been studying the history of the Second World War and researching the role of the RAF in helping Great Britain win the war. Callum found that there were quite a few links to Mull. Bombers that had crashed on the hills and the heroics of some of the pilots that had originated from Mull as well as many others.

There was, however, one story that had really caught his imagination - it was a real modern day mystery but it had its origins going back to World War Two.

Callum had been told of the great Mull mystery of 1975 and it had intrigued him for quite some time. He had often thought about it and wondered what it would be like to solve it! He decided that at their next get-together with his friends he would share the story and seek their help.

He called a meeting that weekend in the usual way by leaving stones on the bridge at the loch and at 3 o'clock that afternoon they all got together. It had been a busy time for them all since their visit to Tobermory but they had still missed one other. They were all a tiny bit excited as every time they got together something seemed to happen to get them into mischief!

Once they had shared stories about what they'd been up to, Callum told them the story of the missing airman from 1975.

"It was Christmas Eve. Peter and Emelia, his fiancée, were enjoying a lovely evening meal at the Killiechron Country House Hotel by the local airfield. They had arrived earlier that day having flown in on a Cessna light aircraft.

They had been to the Isle of Skye as they were thinking of buying a house there. After their meal Peter decided, out of the blue, to take his plane for a short trip around the island before going to bed. After a couple of hours, when Peter hadn't returned, his fiancée called the police and this sparked a massive search of land and sea but there was no trace of him or the plane.

After a couple of days the search was called off. A few days later a wheel from the airplane washed up on the shore by the hotel but there was no sign of the plane. That was the end of the mystery, or so everyone thought.

The plot, however, thickened as 6 months later a farmer, whilst tending his sheep, discovered a body high up on a hill some distance from the airfield. It turned out that the man had died from exposure and it was the body of Peter. What was strange however was there were no signs of any injuries and there was no trace of any salt water on his clothes - that was where the mystery lay, a lot of unanswered questions."

Callum went on to say "It's coming up to the 40th anniversary of the airman's disappearance and wouldn't it be great if we could solve the mystery?"

Whilst they all agreed, it was a very tall order as it happened a very long time ago and none of them had a clue where to start.

Callum was a little disappointed, but wasn't going to give up and said, 'The Gold Bullion mystery happened a lot longer ago than 1975 yet we managed to solve that one!"

They broke up their meeting, agreeing to go away and think about the mystery and would meet again shortly.

That evening, whilst having his tea, Callum's dad started talking to him about the hen harriers. Callum became very interested as their habitat was not far from the airfield.

His dad said "There's a juvenile hen harrier up on the hill past the hotel and I need to go and check up on it sometime."

Callum asked "Can I go with you?"

His dad was pleased at the interest being shown and before he could reply, Callum said, "Can we go tomorrow?"

His dad wondered what the rush was but nonetheless agreed, even if he failed to realise that Callum had an ulterior motive.

Callum was up early to do all his chores (feed the dog, empty the dishwasher, tidy his bedroom, do his homework) so that his dad could have no excuses for not taking him to Maol Buidhe. Later that morning they left and on their way they popped in to the coffee shop to pick up coffees (and some of Laura's delicious chocolate brownie!) as they both thought that they'd need some provisions.

They called at the local shop to pick up a paper and they went along the road to Craignure. Just past Glenforsa they took a forest track up to Maol Buidhe.

They parked up and then tucked into their coffee and cake before putting on their coats, picking up their binoculars and walking up the hill.

On the way, Callum's dad started talking about the birds "The hen harriers have been really active but I've heard that the juvenile has not been seen now for over a week. I'm worried that something may have happened to him."

Whilst Callum was worried about the bird as well, he was equally interested in the great Mull air mystery!

As they continued their climb up Maol Buidhe, Callum asked his dad about the airplane crash. "Dad, isn't this the hill where the pilot was found?"

His dad was surprised that Callum knew about the mystery and played it down "What pilot are you talking about?" he replied.

"You know, the one that was found on the hill by the farmer?" said Callum.

"Oh, that one" his dad replied. Quite excitedly, Callum jumped in. "Why, how many are there?!"

"There's only been the one as far as I know, but how do you know about that?" his dad said.

"We were talking about the second World War in school and it came up. Wasn't the missing airman a pilot in the war flying Spitfires?" said Callum.

"Now you mention it, I think you're right" his dad said adding, "well, going back to your question, no, the pilot was found on the next hill along – Beinn Chreagach-Mhor, they are very similar, but don't worry there are no ghosts up here!" Ally was always pulling Callum's leg about ghosts and that their old farmhouse was haunted although neither of them had felt or seen anything, they both agreed that there was one it was very friendly!

Callum couldn't hide his disappointment as he continued his walk up Maol Buidhe, kicking stones and scuffing his boots along the rough path thinking to himself "all that work doing stuff around the house, for what!"

No sooner had the thought entered his mind but his dad said, "Shhhhh.... look up there on the skyline!" Callum raised his binoculars, immediately erasing any thoughts of missing planes and pilots. There he saw the majestic sight of a white-tailed eagle flying back to the loch.

He kept watching and he saw the bird dip each wing in turn. He knew all along that it was Elgol and a warm feeling arose inside himself. Under his breath he said, "Good morning Elgol."

"Sorry what did you say Callum?" His dad said.

"Oh, nothing just talking to myself" he replied.

"Did you see that" his dad said, "never seen that before, did you see him dip his wings, just like pilots did in the war to say hello?"

"Yes Dad, maybe he was saying hello to us" said Callum.

"Maybe he was." said his dad.

The mention of the war again brought Callum back to thinking about the missing pilot and he was thinking, "How can I get Dad to take me up Beinn Chreagach-Mhor?"

Then his dad stopped him in his tracks again, this time pointing to the heather covered slopes in front of them. Callum could see the movement of something swooping and gliding low to the ground. He drew his binoculars swiftly up to his eyes to have a better look. He could see the exquisite markings and really appreciate the graceful way the hen harrier skimmed the tops of the bracken and heather looking for its lunch.

They both watched for what seemed like hours as if time had stood still with such admiration. He felt so lucky to have these special moments with his dad.

Ally then said, "I can't see the female or the juvenile, can you Callum?"

"No I can't." said Callum.

With that they both widened their field of vision scanning the hill in front of them.

His dad said, "There she is, just below that dead tree."

Callum spotted her almost immediately, but then went back to looking for the juvenile, 'I hope nothing dreadful has happened to it,' he thought with a heavy heart.

His spirits were lifted soon after as he spotted the young hen harrier and said.

"Dad, there, look it's just behind the male"

His dad focussed on it and with a relieved tone said "Great spot son, I'm glad you came with me. I'm not sure I'd have spotted that. You've got terrific eyesight, well done!"

Callum felt so proud and thought that the trip had not been in vain after all. He carried on watching the juvenile and almost forgot all about the parents. As he continued to follow the juvenile a splash of colour caught his eye and he returned his gaze to focus on it. Just peeping slightly above the bracken was something really dark green, only just visible above the overgrown bracken. Try as he might he couldn't work out what it was.

"Dad" he said, "what's that?"

"Where?" his dad said.

"Just there to the right of the juvenile." Callum said.

"Can't see anything, what are you looking at, is it a bird?" said his Dad.

"No, look at the same level as the bird, scan slowly and there's something dark green peeping out above the bracken." said Callum.

His dad couldn't see what Callum was looking at and Callum was starting to get a bit frustrated as he could see it clearly.

Callum gave instructions again and his Dad said "Got it."

He spent some time studying it and then proceeded to offer an explanation. 'I think it's an old shepherds hut. There are a lot scattered amongst the hills on Mull. Shepherds used to use them during the long winter months to shelter whilst they were tending their sheep.' He added 'Today though they aren't used anymore -

quad bikes have made shepherding a lot easier! In the old days they were quite literally a life saver.'

A life before quad bikes was hard for Callum to imagine!

Callum was intrigued by the hut and as they walked back down Maol Buidhe, both satisfied with their day's work, Callum wondered what stories the hut could hide?

That night, Callum pondered about the air mystery but it seemed like the adventure that they had embarked on was over before it had even started. He'd report back to his friends tomorrow and maybe they'd have to look elsewhere for a mystery to solve - the shepherd's hut may be a good place to start and with that thought swirling around his mind he drifted off to sleep.

The next morning he felt so pleased that he'd done all his chores yesterday. He still had to feed the dog and empty the dishwasher but these he did quickly. He picked up his binoculars and bike and made his way to the bridge alongside the loch where his friends were already waiting. With one voice they all said "You're late!"

Callum responded "It's alright for you, you lot don't have the dishwasher to empty!"

Elgol started, by saying "I saw you Callum, and your dad walking up Maol Buidhe yesterday. Did you recognise me?"

"Of course, I did." said Callum "I'd recognise that crooked beak anywhere, even without your aerobatics!"

Callum said 'The trip was all in vain. It was the wrong hill we'd walked up!'

It seemed to Callum that their attempts to solve the Great Air Mystery had been thwarted.

He then said. "I did, though, spot something that was just as interesting. Dad and I saw an old shepherd's hut."

Elgol, Ella and Callum were quite excited about it and were already hatching a plan to try and find it. Elgol and Ella would take a trip up there to see if they could locate it and check it out. If there was anything to report back on then they would go back up there with Callum.

Callum glanced at Olly and Pollyhannah who were both unusually quiet. "What's the matter?" asked Callum.

"What are we going to do? We can't trek all the way up Maol Buidhe - it's too far for us, and we don't want to be left out" said Olly.

Callum thought for a while and then said "Why don't you and Pollyhannah head off down Loch Ba, then down river Forsa into the Sound of Mull to see what you can find out about the missing plane and we can then meet back at the loch?"

Callum thought to himself that this was a bit of a wild goose chase as the chance of finding anything was remote in the extreme, but at least it would keep Olly and Pollyhannah occupied and involved. Olly and Pollyhannah thought that was a good idea. They agreed that they would all meet together tomorrow morning on what, undoubtedly, was going to be a very tiring day.

The next day Callum told his dad where he was going, and set off to meet his friends at the bridge to plan out their day. Olly and Pollyhannah would head down to the loch and then along the river Forsa which flowed into the Sound of Mull where they would check out the stretch of water by the airfield. Ella had decided to go with them to keep an eye on them. In the meantime, Elgol and Callum would head in the same direction but would investigate the shepherds hut.

Olly and Pollyhannah had been out fishing early on and were quite looking forward to their change of scenery, not to mention they'd heard that there were some very juicy eels in the Sound of Mull! Ella was also partial to an odd eel.

Callum had come prepared with his sandwiches and finding something to eat for Elgol was never a problem! They all agreed to meet up again at the mouth of the loch at 6 o'clock that evening.

Elgol flew off ahead to Maol Buidhe. It didn't take him long to get there and he began circling overhead above the hut. Even with Elgol's eyesight it took him a while to find it as it was almost completely overgrown.

Meanwhile, Callum followed on his bicycle. Elgol couldn't see anything strange from the sky so swooped down to take a closer look - it was all closed up and didn't look like anyone had entered the hut for years. Elgol then flew back to tell Callum what he'd seen.

Once he had reported back they both agreed that there was only one thing for it - they'd have to go into the hut to investigate further.

Elgol led the way and it didn't take long for them to reach the hut. As they got closer though the bracken got higher and higher. Callum had to be very careful with his footing as the ground was very uneven and he could very easily twist an ankle, although he didn't really give it much thought, spurred on by what he might find in the hut.

Callum finally battled his way to the hut as Elgol sat on a nearby rock. Callum hoped that having got this far it wasn't locked, although he did recall his dad saying that they were left open so that anyone in trouble could find shelter there. His dad also said that in the past there were always provisions and a wee bottle of Tobermory whisky for medicinal purposes!

Callum pushed at the door but it seemed to be firmly stuck. He looked around for a lock but there wasn't one so he pushed again. This time it moved slightly, and opened just enough so that he could get his arm in. He tried again but there seemed to be something pressing against the door that was stopping him. He looked around the hut and found a window which he peered through but it was so dirty and dark inside that he couldn't see anything. He tried the door again and with an extra strong push managed to budge the obstruction and he fell inside the hut with an almighty clatter.

On hearing the clatter Elgol flew away in a panic and continued his observation of the hut by circling from a safe distance.

Back in the hut, Callum picked himself up and using the light from his phone started scanning inside the hut. He could see what had been barring the door - it was an old bicycle that was very rusty and covered in cobwebs. It's a good job I'm not afraid of spiders he thought.

On the floor by the bicycle lay a can of blue spray paint. There was a wooden table and chair and a log burning stove and the whole place was covered in a thick layer of dust - it was clear that no one had been inside the hut for a very long time.

Callum carried on looking around and saw an old ruck-sack nestled in the corner. As he went to look more closely he stood on something. He reached down and it was a round metal tag - he picked it up and it had an inscription on it "On hire from Mull Bicycle Hire". He looked at it further and saw that it had come off the bike. Callum thought, looking at the state of the bicycle, that if it had been on hire then someone was going to have a very hefty bill to pay!

He made his way over to the ruck-sack. It was very dirty, the zip was rusty and when he picked it up it was very heavy. Callum's heart missed a beat as he wondered what on earth was inside and what mystery could be unfolding.

He carried the ruck-sack outside and Elgol swooped down to greet him, pleased to see him still in one piece.

Elgol looked up and asked Callum "What have you found, and what was that clatter?"

"It was only an old bike falling over and look at this." Callum said pointing to the old ruck-sack.

Callum so wanted to open it. Ordinarily, he would have left the ruck-sack in the hut but it was clear that whoever's it was wasn't coming back to claim it and the only way he could possibly get it back to its rightful owner would be to open it to try and find out who it might belong to.

They decided to head back down the hill to the loch as it would soon be time to meet up with Olly and Pollyhannah.

The journey down was accomplished in half the time as they looked forward to inspecting the ruck-sack. They hadn't been there long when they saw the familiar ripples in the loch of Olly and Pollyhannah.

Olly and Pollyhannah got out of the loch and came and sat on some rocks by Elgol and Callum. They looked exhausted - Callum felt quite guilty as he hadn't realised just how far the Sound of Mull had been.

Callum could hardly contain himself as he wanted to tell Olly and Pollyhannah about his find but politely asked them "How did you get on?"

Olly perked up. "Well we've had quite a day" he said, "We followed the river down past the airfield and into the sea. We swam around for a while and then came across a school of dolphins. We'd met them before as they were local residents and we'd often spent time playing with them. They also helped Pollyhannah when I was lost in the storm. We asked them about the plane and they said that they were aware of a wreck on the bottom of the sea-bed about a quarter of a mile off the shore."

Olly continued "We told them that we would go and look for it if they could show us the way - but they weren't sure where it was, so they told us to do some fishing and they would go and look and then report back. We were both hungry so didn't take much persuading! After a while they came back and were quite excited - they said that they'd found it, a funny looking boat with what looked like wings, they also said that it had markings on "PT7788". We think this has to be the missing plane."

Polly then said. "We wanted to go and investigate further but we saw the ferry heading down the Sound so knew that it was time to head back to the loch. The wreck isn't going anywhere and we now know where to look for it."

Callum was excited to hear their news and almost forgot about his own adventures especially as he recognised the marking number on the plane as being from the missing aircraft.

Callum then told Olly and Pollyhannah about what he'd found at the hut; the blue bicycle, the metal tag, the can of paint and the ruck-sack!

It was getting late and Callum had told his dad that he'd be back in time for tea so they all agreed that they'd meet up the following day to see what was in the ruck-sack.

Callum got home and placed the ruck-sack in the shed with his bike. He went to help his dad get the tea, but couldn't stop thinking about what they had discovered and wondering what it could all be about. Over tea, Callum talked to his dad about Mull bike hire.

"Dad?" he said, "How long has 'Roddy the bike-man' been doing bike hire?"

"That's a strange question" said his Dad. "I don't really know. It's a very long time as I can remember his father used to run it before him." He was quite the pioneer at the time as no one had ever thought about making money from hiring out bikes. I swear that some of the bikes he has now are ones his old dad used to hire out!" "Why do you ask Callum?" he added.

"No reason, just wondering" said Callum.

"Well, while you are still wondering just load the dishwasher with the dishes from tea will you please?" said his dad.

"Okay" said Callum.

"Now this was strange." Callum's dad thought, "this is the first time that Callum has loaded the dishwasher without a little moan!"

Callum completed the job, all the time thinking about the hut. He also told himself that before he met up with his friends, he would pay his friend Roddy a visit at Mull bike hire to see what he could find out.

The next day, Callum got up and cycled to see Roddy the bike-man. Roddy was just opening the shop up and gave Callum a warm smile and said a hearty "hello" adding "How are you today, how's Mull's youngest BCS warden?"

"I'm fine, thank you Roddy. Have you got a minute I just wanted to ask you something?" replied Callum.

"Always got time for you" said Roddy "but I've got some holiday makers coming in to collect five bikes so we'll have to chat as I work, if you don't mind?"

"No, that's fine, let me help you" said Callum.

Callum had helped at the bike shop before so knew what to do and started putting together the packs - helmets, maps, puncture repair kits, pumps and ruck-sacks. It was then that he noticed that the bag with the bicycle spanners was an old ruck-sack that looked remarkably like the one he'd found in the hut.

Callum asked his friend "How long's the shop been here Roddy and when was the business started?"

Roddy replied "Well Callum, as a business we'll be celebrating fifty years this year and we're planning a special celebration at the local hotel for customers old and new as well as local people."

Callum asked Roddy "do bikes ever go missing?"

Roddy said "Very rarely. I take a deposit and being an island, if one ever went missing then all I'd have to do is report it to the police and they'd just wait by the ferry terminal at Craignure to catch the thief. They'd be easy to spot as all my bikes are painted red and our metal tags are riveted onto the frame."

Immediately, this made Callum think of the bicycle in the hut - the blue can of paint and the metal tag. It looks as if the bicycle was one of Roddy's (or his fathers), but why would anyone want to steal a bicycle?

Callum waved Roddy goodbye and headed back to the loch to meet up with his friends and tell them what else he'd found out - the plot was beginning to thicken!

His friends were all sat under the bridge waiting for Callum, and, more importantly, the ruck-sack. Callum knew that they were all desperate to see what was in the ruck-sack and even though he felt the same, he let the tension mount by telling them about his earlier conversation with Roddy. They all thought it very strange.

It wasn't long before Elgol lost patience and said,

"For goodness sake, Callum will you please open the ruck-sack!"

Callum slowly opened the rusty zip, it took some manoeuvring as it hadn't been opened for a very long time. His friends all edged forward to get a better look in the bag and slowly Callum began to remove the contents.........

A metal biscuit tin with a picture of a deer advertising Scottish shortbread -surely there couldn't be any biscuits inside and even though he was rather peckish, he didn't fancy eating one even if there was!

There were several notebooks all bundled together with a piece of grey ribbon.

There was an envelope with something in and some keys.

I wonder who this belongs to, thought Callum, but clearly after all this time whoever it belonged to, they had not bothered to go and retrieve it.

Callum opened the envelope and in it was a passport with an old photograph in and the name of Ethan Gatward. So that was who the ruck-sack belonged to but who was he?

In the envelope alongside the passport was some money - it had decayed quite badly and it looked like some of the money was foreign, there was a lot of it though.

Then Callum turned his attention to the tin. It was very rusty and as he tried to prise the lid off by getting a fingernail under the lip of the lid, his nail broke, at the same time as the lid flew off making a clatter as it landed on the rocks beside them. As quick as a flash, Olly and Pollyhannah darted into the water as the sound scared the living daylights out of them. It was a good couple of minutes before they surfaced from the water - their little excursion was not in vain as they both had a crab in their mouths!

Meanwhile, unflinchingly Elgol and Ella had remained motionless giving Olly and Pollyhannah a funny look and a roll of their eyes.

The tin contained all sorts of what could best be described as trinkets. There was a watch, a ring, some cufflinks with Spitfires on, a pen and what looked like a woman's wedding ring - all very personal items. Why on earth would all these things be in a biscuit tin in an old hut halfway up a mountain on Mull, and why had no one come to retrieve them?

Callum then turned his attention to the bundle of notebooks. It was getting late, as he'd promised to help his dad on the farm so he told his friends that he would take them home and see what they contained and report back tomorrow. In the meantime, they tried to make sense of what they had found but none of them could come up with a logical explanation.

Olly said "Tomorrow we'll head back out early to go and take another look at the sunken airplane to see if we can find any clues as to what has happened. We'll see you back under the bridge at 6 o'clock."

Callum said "Ok, I'll examine the notebooks and report back."

Meanwhile, Elgol and Ella said they would go back up to the hut to see if they'd missed anything from the day before and to show Ella where the hut was.

They could all sense that the mystery was starting to unfold and I think they all felt that there was a link between their findings and the missing plane but what could that link be?

Callum got home, helped his dad and after tea told him he was going to have an early night to catch up on some reading relating to his school project.

He took the notebooks from the ruck-sack with him and, once in his pyjamas, gently took the ribbon off the books and carefully opened the first one.

The notebook was the size of a diary and was written in very neat writing. The pages had become discoloured over time and were a yellowy colour. Although for their age, the book was in very good condition.

Very gently he turned the first page and started reading.

"It's starting again. It's been such a long time since I've had these feelings, I thought they'd gone.

My first recollections of these feelings went back to Benjamin, my lovely pet rabbit. Benjamin had been a birthday present from my Uncle John. Uncle John was your typical animal lover - if he saw an injured bird on the road he'd pick it up and look after it. My favourite memory of Uncle John was when he found an abandoned fox cub on the side of the road. He nursed it back to health but because the cub had to have 24-hour care, he used to take it to work with him in Liverpool - his secretary soon had another additional chore - bottle feeding the cub!

I was very attached to Benjamin and we were inseparable. One night I had a bad dream that Benjamin had been taken ill in the night. When I woke up I rushed downstairs and was horrified to find that Benjamin was dead in his hutch - this was the start of it.

All the time, whilst at school, these negative thoughts kept coming into my mind.

Fearing I'd have a puncture in my bicycle tyre, playing football and missing a penalty, falling down the stairs and breaking my arm, my parents divorcing. These "coincidences" kept on happening and I soon convinced myself that I was to blame for everything bad that happened to my nearest and dearest and me.

I tried to stop these thoughts, I could sense them coming as a feeling of dread and doom washed over me - when it did I would stop what I was doing and do something completely different such as playing the piano or even pinching myself.

For a while this seemed to stop these bad thoughts and it appeared as if I could control the situation by this diversion strategy until one night I had a bad dream again - that my sister was seriously ill. I dreaded waking up the following morning and when I finally got out of bed my mummy put her arms around me, with tears in her eyes, finally managing to tell me that Anne had been taken ill in the night, was rushed to hospital, but had sadly passed away. I was distraught and once more the feelings of guilt returned.

I began to drift back into my shell, afraid to go out, afraid to play with my friends for fear of what might happen to them. My grand-mother, who I loved dearly, spent a lot of time with me and we shared a lot of our thoughts. I finally plucked up the courage to tell her about my worries and concerns. I thought she would laugh at me, tell me not to be so stupid, but quite the contrary. She told me that ever since she was a little girl, she had had the same thoughts and she recounted similar tales to me of bad things happening. Her father's hand getting caught in a machine at work, her swing breaking, cakes burning and she even confided in me that she had had the same dream about my dear, dear sister Anne.

I was so relieved to find that someone shared my secret and that she understood. We talked for hours and I asked her how she coped and how she had learnt to live with these feelings.

She told me of the strategy that she had adopted which very much mirrored mine - diversion tactics. Every time a horrible thought came into her mind she would do something to prove the premonition wrong, so if she thought she'd burn a cake she would bake a cake but make sure it didn't burn, even if it meant that the cake wasn't even cooked. Gradually, the feelings subsided and the premonitions became rarer and rarer.

I tried similar tactics again and gradually the feelings went away, or so I thought.

As the second World War progressed I enlisted into the RAF, originally as ground crew, but as the war went on and the casualties rose, the opportunity arose for me to train as a pilot. I was a natural and I had really found my calling in life. I relished the chance to take to the skies. Alone in the plane I felt invincible and soon chalked up plenty of hours and became a bit of a star in the squadron.

As my friends got killed in the war the feelings of dread and doom returned and I could feel myself getting sucked into a downward spiral again. As time went on, I thought that it was only a matter of time before I had that feeling about one of my friends. It was then that I remembered my grand-mother's cake. I soon felt that a spitfire would crash - not knowing whether it was a friend or myself and deep down hoping it would be me so as to spare one of my friends. I went out onto the airfield and approached the ground crew. I explained that I needed to have a test flight around the airfield as I could feel something loose with the rudder control. In reality it was to prove my feeling of impending disaster wrong. This became a regular occurrence and whilst people thought I didn't know, most people at the airfield referred to me as "petrified Pete" but I didn't mind just as long as my friends remained safe. I managed to get through the war pretty much unscathed and I finally thought that my premonitions had been firmly put to bed.

Years passed, and my life was pretty boring albeit very successful as I was building up a sizeable property portfolio. It was then that I met up with Emelia. Emelia was an old school friend and she was my first true love even though she hadn't realised it! We'd not seen each other over the years and she had married but had become widowed in the war.

It was pure coincidence how we met, bumping into each other leaving Barclays Bank in Market Drayton.

We decided to go for coffee. We chatted away for hours, during which we rekindled our feelings for each other. The romance blossomed, but as it did, so the premonitions returned. I recall one time driving along and a thought came into my mind that I would have a puncture. I slowed down and, five minutes down the road, I felt the car veer suddenly to the left. I pulled over and looked at the tyre - it was flat!

My love for Emelia grew and grew and it was only a matter of time before I popped the question. I was over the moon when she accepted and we then started planning our future life together.

I tried to hide the instances of my dreadful thoughts putting them down to coincidences but they were becoming more and more frequent and I was getting more and more worried. I knew that I had to do something. I couldn't bear it if one of these thoughts involved any harm coming to Emelia."

This was all very intriguing to Callum and he didn't quite understand what this had to do with the missing plane. He turned over the pages and came across the following….

Checklist

Passport

Money

Bicycle

Ferry times

Map of Mull

Dry-sack

Spare clothes

Letter to Emelia

Callum didn't know what this meant and he knew that he would have to share his findings with his dad.

Callum struggled to get to sleep as he couldn't stop thinking about what he had read. Eventually, as he tried to put the jigsaw pieces together, he drifted off to sleep.

The following day, Olly and Pollyhannah got up early and made their way down to the Sound of Mull. They soon found the sunken aircraft and spent some time swimming in and out of the plane.

It was half covered in silt as, over the years, the sea-bed had started to engulf the plane. They could see that one of the wheels was missing, presumably the one washed up on the shore all those years ago. Olly searched the cock-pit and found what looked like a ruck-sack - he tried to pull it out but it was stuck behind the seat and try as they might they couldn't budge it. They then both headed to shore.

They caught their breath and then headed back to the loch. They all met up under the bridge – they had a lot to report.

Callum told them about the notebooks, what had been written and the check list. They were all puzzled as to what it meant.

Olly then told them about the plane, how it was lying on the seabed and the ruck-sack that they had found.

Callum now had no alternative but to tell his dad about what he'd found when he got home.

When he got home his dad was sat in the living room reading a book about hen harriers. He looked up and could see a puzzled look on Callum's face.

"What's up Callum, you look worried?" his dad said.

"I am Dad, I've found something and I don't know what to do?" Callum said, starting to bite his finger-nail. His dad knew something was wrong as Callum only did this when he was in trouble or worried.

"Come over here and tell me all about it. What's that you've got there?" his dad said softly.

Callum sat down by his dad and told him the whole story, how he'd been back up to the shepherd's hut, about the bicycle, the paint and the Mull bike hire tag. He then told him about the ruck-sack and everything that was in it. At the same time he opened the ruck-sack and the tin showing him what he'd found.

His dad spent time looking at all the items and then said, "I'm

not sure what all this means but first thing in the morning we'll need to go and see my friend PC Birkin at Tobermory police station as there is something strange going on here."

Callum knew that his dad would know what to do and he felt mightily relieved having got this huge weight off his chest. There was something else he needed to tell his dad but he didn't quite know how to tell him but he knew he'd have to share his secret with him.

"Daaaad" he said, "There's something else I need to tell you"

"What's that?" his dad said.

Callum sheepily said "Well you know the two otters that rescued me from the loch last summer in the storm?"

"Yes" his dad said, wondering that this had to do with the shepherd's hut.

"Well, those two otters are my friends, Olly and Pollyhannah, and ever since then we've been playing together. Well, they've found something too"

His dad looked a bit surprised but not as shocked as Callum thought he'd be.

"I thought as much, I've seen you down the loch playing with them" said his dad.

It was now Callum's turn to look surprised "There's no hiding things from you is there Dad?" he replied.

He went on to tell his dad about the missing plane that they'd found, as well as the ruck-sack in the plane. His dad looked a bit puzzled as to how two otters could have done all that but had no doubt that Callum was telling the truth as he'd never told lies before.

They went to bed wondering what tomorrow would bring with Callum's dad thinking about how he was going to explain the finding of the plane and the ruck-sack that Olly and Pollyhannah had found.

The next day, they set off early to Tobermory to go and see PC Birkin.

Ally had rung through earlier to make sure that PC Birkin was going to be there. They greeted each other warmly as they were both old school friends. At school they were both going to be policemen, things though didn't quite go according to plan for Ally.

They sat down in an interview room where Callum told PC Birkin the story. PC Birkin took notes all the time and when he finished, he started scratching his head not quite knowing what to make of it all. Ally then chipped in that this might have something to do with the missing plane. PC Birkin thought that was a bit of a leap of faith - but noted the comment down in his notebook.

He told them both to wait in the interview room as he'd have to call this in to the police station in Oban because this was way outside his experience.

It seemed ages before PC Birkin returned and he looked flustered.

He said. "They're sending over a detective and another officer on the next ferry and they want to speak to you both. Can you be back here for two o'clock? In the meantime, please don't discuss this with anyone else."

They readily agreed and decided to head off to the coffee shop for a well-earned lunch before heading back to Tobermory.

They got back to Tobermory just before two o'clock and outside the station was a white police Range Rover - a strange vehicle to the island. Ally said "They must be here."

They met the two officers and went through the whole story again this time concluding by signing statements.

The detective said. "We'll be opening up an investigation, Ally would you please show us where the shepherds hut is?"

Ally said "Yes of course, I'll drop Callum off with Laura at the coffee shop on the way." Callum insisted that he go with them and surprisingly the police officers agreed.

They turned off the road up to Maol Buidhe and, as they made their way up the track, Callum pointed out the hen harrier family hunting over the bracken, up on the skyline. Callum saw Elgol and Ella keeping their beady eyes on them.

They made their way up to the hut and it was clear that the detectives hadn't planned on an excursion up a mountain as their shoes would soon be ruined! They reached the hut and the detective said "You two wait here."

It was just as Callum had said. They put on forensic gloves and slowly started to sift through the contents of the hut, taking photographs of everything before touching anything.

It seemed like ages as Callum and his dad waited outside and all that time Elgol sat on a rock, not moving a feather, watching the events unfold. The detectives emerged and placed blue tape all around the hut to prevent anyone from entering. As they made their way back down Maol Buidhe they started getting things moving - it was clear this was to be a major investigation as a policeman was to be dispatched to keep an eye on the hut until forensic scientists arrived.

Callum and his dad then headed home - it had been quite a day. On their way back, Callum said. "What about the plane Dad, how are you going to let the police know about it?"

His dad said "Leave that to me, just make sure that Olly and Pollyhannah meet us on the shore tomorrow morning as they'll need to show me exactly where the plane lies on the bottom of the seabed."

Callum told him that he'd make sure they would be there and headed off to the loch to arrange this with his pals. In the meantime, when Callum's dad got home he rang Malcom at Mull boat hire and arranged to borrow his boat the next day to go and look for basking sharks.

They both slept well and after breakfast they headed off to the harbour at Ulva ferry. There they met Malcolm who handed over the keys to the boat - he also wished them happy hunting and hoped that they find what they were looking for. Callum and Ally hoped so too!

It was quite a trip, one that Ally and Callum had done many times before, but this was perhaps the first time that they actually knew what they were looking for and where it was. It took them a while to get there. They rounded the coastline by the airfield and Callum started scanning the shore looking for Olly and Pollyhannah. It didn't take him long to spot them lying on some kelp eating crabs. Callum started waving and the otters, having recognised his scent, started swimming towards the boat. As they did, Ally turned on the sonar on the boat to try and find the plane. Olly and Pollyhannah swam towards the plane and when they got above it circled over it pointing it out to Callum and his dad.

Callum thought "Where's a submarine when you need it?" thinking back to the submarine used to try and find the Spanish galleon.

Ally picked up the plane on the sonar and knew that this was what they had been looking for. He marked the spot on his sat nav and then they headed back to Ulva ferry. All he had to do now was to persuade the police that finding this on the sonar was a coincidence - no way would anyone believe him that Olly and Pollyhannah had led them there!

The police investigation was really beginning to gather momentum and whilst Callum and Ally had been true to their word by not discussing this with anyone, it didn't take long for the rumours to spread across the island. Various people connected to the investigation had arrived on the island and even reporters from the Oban Times had moved into the Isle of Mull hotel.

The following day, Ally called PC Birkin. "Robert, I've got some further information that I think may be relevant to the investigation."

PC Birkin said "Well that's a coincidence as I was just about to call you. I need you to come into the police station to help us with our enquiries. Can you also bring Callum with you?"

Ally agreed to meet there later that day.

Callum was quite excited to learn what they had found out and also to see how they would react to his dad's discovery of the airplane.

When they got there PC Birkin had been joined by DI Campbell from Oban police station.

DI Campbell said enquiringly "You said that you have some further information for us?"

Ally said. "I've been mapping out white-tailed eagle territories along the sound of Mull for the BCS and at the same time looking for basking sharks by the airfield. Yesterday, I recorded an unusual recording on the sonar that can't be living. I wonder whether it might, just might, be connected to the missing plane all those years ago?"

Ally was very apologetic about sharing this information and hoped he wasn't wasting their time.

PC Birkin and DI Campbell looked quizzically at each other with a knowing look as if it was another piece of the jigsaw taking shape. DI Campbell asked to be excused saying that he needed to make a call.

The call he made was to the police launch and divers that had been drafted in from Oban - it's almost as if they'd had a premonition that they would be required. He gave the police divers the sat nav co-ordinates and they made their way to look for the plane. Meanwhile DI Campbell returned to Callum and Ally.

DI Campbell thanked Ally for the additional information about the possible plane location. DI Campbell then went on to give a brief summary of the investigation to date - it seemed as if there had been many leads to follow up on and that as soon as they had done so they would let them know.

Whilst showing them out PC Birkin asked Ally "Tell me again, just why you happened to be in the Glenforsa area?"

Ally said "I must admit that, whilst we had mainly been looking for white-tailed eagles and basking sharks, we were also looking for any signs of the plane. Callum's been pestering me about it as he's been studying this at school." PC Birkin seemed satisfied with the explanation.

They didn't hear anything for a few more days and Callum was getting frustrated at the lack of news - every day he'd meet his friends at the bridge at the loch and they were getting impatient for news too - what could be taking them so long?

The day finally came when they were called back into the station - they were made welcome and comfortable with drinks. PC BIrkin and DI Campbell called them into the now familiar surroundings of the interview room.

DI Campbell spoke first. "Thanks for coming in today and for all your co-operation." He then went on. "This has been an intricate and complex case not made any easier by the passage of time. You're both correct this whole case is connected with the great Mull air mystery."

He then went on to enlighten them as to what they thought had happened.......

"Peter was a good businessman, a war hero and, to the outside world, a very successful man. This facade though, masked a deeply troubled man who had been plagued by mental illness ever since he was a young boy. You must appreciate that mental illness is more commonly diagnosed now than it was back then. Psychiatric experts, from the evidence that we have provided to them, have retrospectively diagnosed Peter as suffering from 'Premonition Reality Syndrome' - PRS."

DI Campbell explained "In simple terms, someone who suffers from this condition magnifies bad random thoughts that come into their head and they convince themselves that by having these thoughts they turn them into reality. These people believe that they alone are controlling people's destinies and this could get so bad that they even think they can control mechanical events (such as punctures). Whilst the likes of you or I would just put such events down to "bad luck", these thoughts can really take hold of someone."

DI Campbell went on. "The condition becomes heightened when the person is under severe pressure (physically or emotionally) and Peter had suffered with this for years." DI Campbell explained. "We've managed to piece together this profile from the notebooks and it would explain that when life was 'calm' for Peter, he didn't have any episodes.

Peter had come to Mull with his fiancée where he hoped to use his visit to finally bring a conclusion to the torment that he was living, and so he hatched a plan.

Peter loved Emelia so much that it was this emotional high that was triggering his PRS and it was actually making his condition worse. Peter truly believed that it was only a matter of time before he would have a bad thought of harm coming to Emelia and that he would lose her.

Peter came to Mull to say goodbye to Emelia. They'd had an idyllic day flying over the highlands and islands of Scotland. He'd found a house on Skye for Emelia to live in comfortably and they'd rounded the day off with a romantic meal at the Killiechron Country House Hotel.

Life didn't get any better - reports from the time of the missing plane captured how many people had remarked about them being the perfect couple.

Peter's plan was becoming a reality in that they had just experienced the perfect day that he'd been planning for quite some time.

Peter believed that if he stayed with Emelia that some awful fate would befall her, and in order to stop that happening he would have to set her free by letting her believe that he had died.

On a previous trip to Mull alone, he had planned his own downfall. He would take Emelia to Skye to look at a property that he had just bought, this would later become her home - she had previously fallen in love with it on an earlier trip. They would then fly back to Mull and have a final meal where he would savour the last few hours of her company. After dinner, he would make an excuse to take the plane out for a circle of the island (Emelia wouldn't think anything of it as she was aware of his actions in the war). Whilst out, he would ditch the plane in the sea, swim to shore with his sack of dry clothes. There he would change into his dry clothes, walk up Maol Buidhe to the shepherd's hut where he'd left a bike that he'd hired (but not returned) from Mull bike hire. He would then assume a new identity (hence the passport), cycle to the ferry terminal the next morning and start his new life as Ethan Gatward.

Emelia would be better off without him and he would make his way in the world with whatever was thrown at him - in this way at least Emelia would be safe and well provided for."

DI Campbell added. "Whilst the plan was well thought out things did not go according to plan. After dinner, it seemed that Peter's mood did change, and, from reports from Emelia and others, he became extremely anxious and concerned. Experts believe that his PRS was kicking in and they feel that he may well have been having terrible thoughts about a disaster striking. Little did he know that the premonition would affect him not Emelia.

Peter took off alright and, once out of sight of the airfield, he brought the plane down to ditch in the sea.

He'd done this several times during the war but I guess he must have been a little rusty. It was dark, the sea choppier than he'd imagined, and it turned out to be a heavier landing than he'd planned. With that, pathologists believe that when he landed he may well have hit his head in the cockpit and suffered from concussion - he may even have blacked out for a while. We believe he managed to get himself out of the plane and swim to shore but he forgot to take his dry-sack of clothes with him to change into. Once ashore he knew that he had to make his way up Maol Buidhe to the shepherd's hut to pick up the bicycle and assume his new identity. Sadly, when ashore he must have been confused, cold and very wet and by mistake climbed Beinn Chreagach-Mhor where he must have collapsed and died of hypothermia leaving his belongings in the hut untouched for all those years."

DI Campbell then said. "We did find the plane exactly where you said it was. Inside we found the sack of clothes and we also found a letter in it addressed to Emelia which was effectively a suicide note that he was going to post when he'd swum ashore. It being a Bank Holiday no one would know that it had been posted after his assumed death."

DI Campbell paused and both Callum and Ally had a tear in their eye - what a sad story for all concerned.

Ally then asked. "What about the paint for the bicycle?"

Before DI Campbell could respond Callum jumped in. "I can answer that - all the bicycles from Mull bike hire are painted red, so Peter needed to paint it blue so as not to arouse suspicion when boarding the ferry, just in case the police were still looking for it."

DI Campbell was most impressed and told Callum that they would make a detective out of him yet!

Callum then asked the detective "But what about the clothes, there were no traces of saltwater on them?"

The detective replied, "There are no flies on you are there Callum? You're right, we think that over the weeks and months that the body was on the mountain the rain had washed the saltwater out of them - that's what the scientists now think."

It came to light, that whilst Emelia did move to the Isle of Skye into the house that Peter had bought for her, she sadly became something of a recluse and only some two years later she died, many say of a broken heart. The saddest thing was not knowing anything of what had now been discovered.

"Well that's some story!" Callum thought and he couldn't wait to enlighten his friends.

Soon this would be all over Mull and once again Callum would be in the limelight.

Before they left the police station, Callum asked DI Campbell.

"What's going to happen to the bicycle?"

DI Campbell said "We've no longer got a need for it. By rights it should be returned to Mull bike hire. However, given the state of it, I don't really think they'll want it back."

Callum asked. "Is it okay if I have it then?"

DI Campbell agreed saying "finders-keepers!"

They left the police station with the bicycle and already there were several news reporters who had gathered all wanting to interview Callum to find out what had happened. Callum though wanted to let Peter and Emelia rest in peace in the hope that they were now reunited.

Some weeks later Callum and Ally made their way to the local hotel to help 'Roddy the bike-man' and his dad celebrate their fifty years in business. Callum went to the back of their Landrover and pulled out what appeared to be a brand new shiny red bicycle.

Between the two of them, Callum and Ally had renovated the bicycle from the hut back to its former glory and they presented it to Roddy and his dad - they were both very pleased to have it back. It now takes pride of place in the shop window and every year 'Roddy the bike-man' uses it in the annual cycle marathon around Mull. If you see him be sure to give him a wave!

Chapter Seven - The Mull Epidemic

Spring was slowly turning into summer on Mull after a very long, cold, hard winter when many of the animal residents of the island feared that they wouldn't make it. But, make it they had, and there was a real sense of optimism as the fields turned green and new born were establishing themselves in the world and looking forward to experiencing life on Mull.

Callum and his friends were looking forward to the summer holidays which were now only weeks away and they were already thinking about what mischief they could get up to and what mysteries needed solving.

Unbeknown to them, and in fact all the residents on Mull, a large black cloud was about to descend upon them!

For Ally this was a very busy time of the year. He was keeping an eye on various habitats, helping with schools and preparing for the huge influx of tourists, made even greater by the reduction in ferry charges. As well as all this he had the farm to look after.

White-tailed eagles are synonymous with Mull, so this was always a key focus for Ally, and every day he made a point of calling to see the Muileach family of white-tailed eagles at Kilbeg.

As the days passed, he started to sense that something wasn't quite right, particularly with the female. Every day he looked but couldn't spot what the problem was.

After a few days more he thought that he would film the white-tailed eagle and then he'd be able to study the footage once he got home. This he did over a week and in addition he went to check on the white-tailed eagles in the Tall Trees Again he could tell that there was something wrong but couldn't spot what.

One evening, Ally downloaded all of the film footage onto his laptop to start studying them in more detail. Callum, who had just finished his home-work, came into his dad's study and said, "What are you doing Dad, I thought it was only me that stared at computer screens?"

Ally said, "Very funny! Look, I've been filming these white-tailed eagles and something's wrong but I can't put my finger on what it is."

They watched the videos over and over again and Callum agreed with his dad that something wasn't quite right but neither could say what it was.

Callum then suggested to his dad. "Why don't you look at the very first video and then compare it to the last one as any differences will be more noticeable?"

"That's a great idea Callum." said his dad.

After flicking backwards and forwards several times Callum said, "Look Dad, on the first one Rona, (realising he'd called the eagle by name and quickly correcting himself), sorry, I mean the eagle, flies straight back to the branch where she came from but on the last video when she gets back she doesn't seem to know which one it is and looks confused?"

His dad agreed and ran the videos through again, "Also, look at the angle she's coming in to the trees. It's all wrong and not normal. It's a wonder she hasn't crashed into those branches."

Callum became more and more concerned for his friends as he realised that something was clearly very wrong with Rona! His dad then studied the other videos from the Tall Trees and similar things were happening there - this wasn't an isolated incident. Callum then spotted, in the distance, on one of the videos something that looked even stranger.

"Dad, look there over those trees – zoom in." said Callum. His dad did and they saw a white-tailed eagle but it was flying upside down!

They knew that they did this in courtship and to transfer food but they'd never seen anything quite like this before - something was very clearly amiss.

The next day, Ally left to check on the other white-tailed eagles right across the island to see if he could find any other examples of this strange behaviour. As he drove, thoughts whirled around in his mind "Was it behavioural? Was it an illness? Or even was he just imagining it!"

Meanwhile, Callum hot-footed it down to the bridge at the loch to meet his friends, having already left stones there the day before. They all arrived and clearly very pleased to see each other - they too were looking forward to playing together now that the warmer weather and lighter nights were here.

Callum soon started talking about what his dad and he had identified the night before but tactfully as he didn't want to alarm Elgol.

He said casually. "How's Rona these days?"

Elgol then said. "Well actually, she's not been her usual self – she's been very quiet, has started to miss a few fish when fishing and perhaps more worryingly hasn't nagged me to tidy the nest now for over a week – something's clearly up!"

Callum was careful not to alarm Elgol and decided not to tell him about his concerns, especially until he'd spoken more to his dad to see whether he'd had any ideas. Off they all went as they all had chores to do and they agreed to meet up the following day.

Ally had toured the island, and, now that he knew what he was looking for, had spent the day becoming increasingly more concerned as he saw more evidence of strange behaviours in the white-tailed eagle population - it was clear that what he'd seen previously was not an isolated incident.

On his way home he called the BCS vet in Glasgow – Jeremy - and explained to him what he'd seen.

Jeremy said. "I've not encountered anything like this before." Sensing the concern in Ally's voice he agreed to visit Mull the following day and Ally said that he'd meet him from the mid-day ferry at Craignure. This gave Ally a degree of comfort in knowing that someone was taking his concerns seriously, and he couldn't have anyone better than Jeremy to help him.

That night, Ally told Callum all about his day and told him about his concerns and this made Callum even more fretful for Elgol and Rona. Could she be infected or suffering from whatever was affecting the white-tailed eagles? If she was, would Elgol catch it? Would they find a cure?

The following day Ally was woken up very early by the phone ringing. It was PC Birkin from Tobermory. They'd found a dead white-tailed eagle in fields just outside Dervaig, with no apparent cause. He agreed to drop it off with Ally later that morning.

No sooner had he put the phone down than it rang again. This time it was Howard, the game-keeper from an estate on the south of Mull. He too had found a dead white-tailed eagle under similar circumstances. Howard said he'd drop the bird off later that morning too. Ally was now very worried and needed help more than ever - was this purely coincidence or was there something more sinister happening?

PC Birkin and Howard both arrived at the same time from different ends of the island to be greeted by Callum who wasn't aware of the conversations that they'd had with his dad. He was shocked to hear what had happened and quickly made his excuses as he needed to see his friends as soon as possible. His dad met PC Birkin and Howard and heard about the circumstances in which both birds had been found. He placed them in boxes in his freezer in the garage and then left to meet Jeremy off the ferry at Craignure.

He got to the ferry terminal and spoke to Franky from the ferry company who told him that the ferry had been delayed, so to pass the time they went for a coffee and a quick sandwich. Ally sensed that when he picked up Jeremy the afternoon would soon fly by! They soon saw the Isle of Mull ferry just coming round the headland past Duart Castle at which point Franky ran out of the shop and along the pier just ready to catch one of the ship's ropes in the nick of time!

Meanwhile, Ally left the coffee shop at a more leisurely pace, making his way across the road as the passengers were disembarking from the ferry. He watched carefully, trying to guess which one looked like a BCS vet. Several people walked past him that he thought they could be but then he spotted a young man with jeans, a tee shirt and a ruck-sack with a BCS waterproof in his hand. Clearly this was Jeremy. He introduced himself and they walked back to the Land-rover together.

Ally then said. "There's been further bad news I'm afraid – two white-tailed eagles have been found dead at opposite ends of the island with no apparent cause."

Jeremy said "We'd better carry out a post-mortem to see if we can find out what has caused their deaths – do you have access to a vet's operating theatre so that we can examine the birds?"

Ally called Cameron the local vet. Ally explained what had happened and Cameron offered any help he could and advised the theatre would be free later that afternoon to use.

Meanwhile, Callum was meeting up with his friends at the loch, and he had the bad news to report of the two dead white-tailed eagles. Elgol turned white as his thoughts turned to the loss of his father. He also thought that his mother might be ill although he had no fear for himself. Everyone tried to console Elgol, and vowed to do anything they could to help find out what the problem was.

Callum went on to explain what his dad and he had seen by observing the white-tailed eagles, as they tried to make sense of what was happening to the famous birds of Mull.

Olly and Pollyhannah looked at each other with tears in their eyes as they both cast their minds back to when they lost their mum and dad. There was something in what they'd heard from Callum that was ringing a bell.

Callum asked. "Are you two ok?"

Pollyhannah replied. "This reminds us of what happened to our parents. The illness had crept up on them very quickly. One day they were as right as rain and then weeks later they both passed away. Initially, they couldn't hold their breath as long as usual, they lost their sense of direction and became clumsy and started bashing into things. They gradually became more and more poorly until finally they passed away."

Both Olly and Pollyhannah were now in tears. Callum enquired, sensitively. "Do you know what they'd died of?"

Olly said. "Our grandparents had a theory that it was related to the Scottish midge. They said that otters very rarely catch diseases from them but there's one that, if contracted, was incurable. It was very rare, especially as midges don't normally bother otters as they don't share the same habitat and the midges struggle to penetrate the thick wet skins of an otter."

It seemed like Olly and Pollyhannah's parents were therefore extremely unlucky for both of them to suffer in this way.

This got Callum thinking that maybe, just maybe, the white-tailed eagles were suffering from the same fate as Olly's parents - he would discuss this with his dad when he got home.

Back at Callum's home, Ally and the BCS vet Jeremy had examined the dead white-tailed eagles and Jeremy couldn't find any obvious indicators as to what fate had befallen them. Jeremy wanted to see their habitat, so they drove up to Dervaig and walked to where the white-tailed eagle had been found. There was nothing obvious that gave any clue as to why the white-tailed eagle had died but they were plagued by the famous Scottish midges all the time – a new experience for Jeremy.

They then made their way down to the south of the island past Pennyghael and met Howard who took them up the hill on quad bikes to where he'd found his casualty. It took them about twenty minutes to get there with Howard and Ally laughing at Jeremy slapping himself across the face trying to keep the midges at bay. Howard gave him a spray of Old Musk telling him that it was the best midge repellent ever invented. Again, there was nothing obvious that would cause injury to the white-tailed eagles from the two habitats that they'd visited.

Jeremy concluded that they needed to get back to the vet's practice so that he could carry out the post-mortems on the two birds. When they got there, they were made very welcome by Cameron the vet. He was very worried about these latest events and was concerned that if there was an illness affecting the island's white-tailed eagles, whilst this was a disaster in itself, there was always a chance that it could spread to other animals.

Cameron offered to assist Jeremy with the examination and they did a full post mortem but couldn't find anything to tell them what had caused their deaths. They under-took full blood analysis and toxicology tests but they wouldn't get the results back for a few days in normal circumstances. But they both knew that time was against them.

Cameron had an idea. He wanted to go and see the owner of the fish farm – Fred. He told the others to leave it with him. How knowing the owner of the fish farm could help remained a mystery to the others!

Cameron rang through to Fred after he'd noticed the helicopter that regularly transports salmon heading to the fish farm earlier in the day. Cameron explained the position to him and the seriousness of the situation. Fred agreed and gave instructions for their helicopter to be scrambled to pick up the blood samples from Mull and take them to the laboratories in Glasgow.

It landed on the rugby pitches just outside Craignure and Cameron and Jeremy were there to meet them with the blood samples. The rotor blades whirred into action again and, with the blink of an eye, the helicopter was heading off into the distance over to Oban and beyond to Glasgow where the scientists would do their work to try and find out what had caused the death of the white-tailed eagles.

It had been quite an adventurous day. Jeremy had been planning on catching the last ferry from Craignure back to Oban but, with events taking a turn for the worse, it was clear that his work on Mull was only just beginning.

Jeremy said. "I'll book into the Hotel in Craignure."

Ally, though, said insistently. "No, you must stay with us. I won't hear of it, we've got plenty of room and it will be good company for Callum. We've still got lots to talk about."

Jeremy readily agreed as he spent a lot of his life in hotel rooms and much preferred home comforts.

They arrived back home where Callum was eagerly waiting for any news. Before they could speak Callum asked them. "Did you see that helicopter flying over - I wonder where it's been and where it was going. It was very low."

Ally said. "That's one mystery that I can solve!" and then went on to tell him about Cameron the vet and the strings that he'd pulled to get the blood test results back as soon as possible. Callum was impressed and relieved that this problem was being dealt with urgently.

Over dinner Callum continued grilling Jeremy. "Did you see anything suspicious from your trips to Dervaig or Pennyghael? Did the post-mortems show anything? Have you seen anything like this before?"

The questions kept coming until Ally stepped in and said. "That's enough Callum, Jeremy has had a very long day and must be extremely tired. You'll have plenty of time in the morning to continue your interrogation over breakfast!"

Reluctantly, Callum said "Sorry and Goodnight." He made his way to bed wondering whether he should say something to Jeremy over breakfast about Olly and Pollyhannah's parents and how they'd died.

Ally and Jeremy went through to the living room where two wee drams of Tobermory 15 year-old malt whisky were poured whilst they wondered what could be affecting the white-tailed eagles. This was quickly followed by two more before they retired to bed, both feeling that tomorrow was going to be a stressful day, even if only answering all of Callum's questions!

In Glasgow, the scientists had been working through the night running tests and analyzing the blood samples from the two post-mortems as they were aware of the urgency of having the results.

At 7 o'clock the next morning Ally's mobile rang, number unknown. He looked at his phone thinking that for anyone to ring at this time of the morning it must be serious. It was Simon, a researcher from the laboratories in Glasgow with the results of the tests. He'd tried Cameron but couldn't get hold of him and Jeremy didn't have a signal. Ally passed over his phone to Jeremy who'd just got back to the farm having taken a walk down by the loch.

The phone call had woken Callum up and he too was listening intently at his bedroom door. It was difficult for him to make any sense of the one-sided call that he'd heard so, when the call ended, he bounded down the stairs to ask his dad who had been on the phone.

Ally said to Callum, "The call was for Jeremy and it was private."

Jeremy jumped in and said. "It's not a secret; we need all the help that we can get."

His dad said to Callum "Go and get washed and dressed - breakfast will be ready in five minutes and you can continue the discussion then."

Callum was ready in a jiffy and in less than two minutes was sat at the kitchen table – Ally said, "It's a pity you don't get ready for school with such enthusiasm!"

They all tucked into their bacon rolls and coffee.

Jeremy then said "The results from the dead white-tailed eagles have come back from Glasgow. The one thing that it did prove was that there was no question of any poison or drugs involved."

This was a huge relief to both Callum and his dad. Deep down they had both feared the worst, particularly knowing what had happened to Elgol's father.

Ally said, "If it wasn't poison then what could have killed them?"

Jeremy replied "There were no signs of any injuries but the blood tests did show that there was some infection that the scientists hadn't seen before in birds and that they would have to run further tests."

It was at this point that Callum thought he had nothing to lose by talking about the otter deaths.

He said to Jeremy, "I've heard about otters dying from an infection caused by midge bites that disorientates them. It affects their breathing and ultimately results in a slow and painful death."

Ally then said "These stories are thought to be old wives' tales and that locally it had been referred to as Squiffy Otter disease. When otters have been spotted, that had subsequently died, people had likened them to being drunk."

Jeremy though wanted to know more, and said "Nothing is making any sense and any thoughts or theories need to be thoroughly checked out."

They spoke about it further and Jeremy phoned Simon back in Glasgow and discussed it further with him. He agreed to run tests to see whether a disease caused by an infection from a midge bite might just have anything to do with the deaths. He would get back to him as quickly as possible. Jeremy told him that time was of the essence and they agreed to speak later that morning.

Ally then recalled that there was a bio-chemist living temporarily at Gribun in a holiday cottage that she was renting over the summer. She had taken some time off to work on a thesis about diseases in birds and had made contact with him already.

"Might she be able to help?" Ally thought. "What was her name?"

He looked in his phone and there it was, yes, Emma, that was it. He gave her a call and as soon as he'd mentioned what happened he could sense the excitement in her voice – yes, she'd be delighted to help and Ally agreed to pick her up in ten minutes to go down and discuss the position with Cameron.

They all met at the vet's and told Cameron the outcome of the calls and introduced Emma. In fact, Cameron had already met her and was helping her with her research. She opened her briefcase and started work right away testing the two dead white-tailed eagles.

Meanwhile, Callum headed down to the loch to meet up with his friends to update them.

Straight away, Callum asked Elgol "How's your mum today?"

Elgol said "She's alright, but she's always very good at hiding things from me and not just my birthday presents! I am very worried though as I can tell that she's not well. She's off her food and all she really wants to do is sit on her favourite branch and look down the loch."

They were all very concerned for Elgol and his mum.

Callum then said, "There is some good news. It's not poison and the best scientific minds in Scotland are working on the blood tests. I'm sure that they'll find the cause especially as Olly and Pollyhannah have told them indirectly where to look."

Callum added "I need to get back to my dad and Jeremy so that I can find out if there have been any developments, I'll let you know what's happening later today."

Back at the vet's, word had spread amongst the community that two white-tailed eagles had been found dead and rumours had been circulating that they'd been poisoned - for many it just seemed the only possible solution. These rumours had reached PC Birkin and he'd made his way to the vets to meet up with Jeremy, Cameron, Emma and Ally. Jeremy explained to PC Birkin that it wasn't poison and whilst he was relieved that he wasn't dealing with any criminal activity he was equally concerned, as he loved the white-tailed eagles as much as anyone on the island. They all agreed to meet up again once they'd heard back from Glasgow. Meanwhile PC Birkin went back to Tobermory to try and quell the poison rumours and he thought the best place to start would be to tell Harry the harbour-master, who could always be found in The Mishnish at this time of day – after he'd told him, PC Birkin knew it wouldn't take long for word to spread!

The next few hours passed very slowly as they all waited for their phones to ring. There were a few false alarms from Uncle Jack and Heather asking for jumble for a Summer Fayre until finally, the call that they'd been waiting for came through on Jeremy's phone.

Ally was listening to the call and he could tell it was a very technical one, so much so, that he struggled to understand some of the language that was used but he did get a sense that they had worked out what the problem was. When the call ended, Callum was the first with the questions.

"Have they found out what caused the deaths?" he blurted out.

"Well, thanks to you, Callum, yes, they have" said Jeremy.

"I don't understand" said Callum "what's it got to do with me?" he added.

"Sit down and I'll explain" said Jeremy.

He said' "The deaths were caused by an infection following a midge bite. Emma and, Simon from the laboratory in Glasgow, have been working together on finding a solution. Emma, with her contacts, referred their findings to the Infectious Diseases Centre in Liverpool and they have confirmed them. The infection causes problems with an animal's or bird's inner ear, so affecting balance, sense of direction and causing animals to become confused and dizzy. The disease becomes so debilitating that, if unchecked, it can lead to death in a matter of weeks, possibly sooner if the animals are incapable of feeding themselves. Up until now the only animals that have been affected (or recorded) have been otters and mink. If it hadn't been for you pointing the scientists in this direction it would certainly have taken longer to have been diagnosed. That is if it would ever be diagnosed at all, as it is so rare."

All this was well and good, but was of no comfort to Callum as he was only concerned with helping to make his friends better.

Callum asked Jeremy, "So, what's the cure?"

Jeremy said "The cure itself is quite simple. It's a very straightforward antibiotic that Cameron has access to in his veterinary surgery."

"That's great," said Callum adding "come on, let's go get it and we can give it to the white-tailed eagles"

"Hold on" said his Dad, "it's not that simple. It's one thing knowing what the problem is, and knowing the cure, but it's another thing getting the cure to the patient and then making sure that the patient takes the medicine! You know how reluctant you are sometimes."

This stopped Callum in his tracks. He'd not given this much thought, what had he been thinking? These eagles are in the remotest parts of the island, they are extremely shy birds and aren't going to put their wing out to allow a vet to give them an injection. Callum felt totally frustrated, he had the cure but could not think of a way to administer the cure to the birds. It was quite a conundrum and he had gone from a feeling of elation to despair in the space of a few moments.

Ally could see this written all over his son's face, and so too could Jeremy.

Ally said, "Right, Jeremy and Callum, you come with me. Meanwhile Cameron, you go to the surgery, collect Emma and the antibiotics and meet us at the Mishnish as soon as you can." It was said in such a tone that no one dared to question these instructions.

Callum, Ally and Jeremy headed off to Tobermory.

"Where are we going?" Callum asked his dad.

"That's a very good question, I was just about to ask myself" said Jeremy.

"We're on our way to see PC Birkin, all will be revealed but I've got an idea!"

The few miles seemed to take an eternity and, clearly Ally was not for sharing his thoughts just yet, so they continued the journey in silence, each looking up to the skies to see if any of them could spot a white-tailed eagle. Callum couldn't imagine Mull without white-tailed eagles and a tear started to roll down his cheek as thoughts of what Elgol must be feeling brought back memories of when his mummy had become very ill before she died.

They arrived at Tobermory police station and waiting outside to greet them was PC Birkin. He said to Ally, "I got your message, everyone will be waiting for us in the Mishnish."

Callum couldn't understand what was going on, but it did look like he would get to go in the Mishnish - an experience he'd not had before! They walked in and the pub was heaving with farmers. Harry the harbourmaster had spread the word amongst the farming community that the white-tailed eagles needed help and that the only people that could save them were the farmers. Upon hearing the cry for help farmers from all over the island had travelled far and wide to help - having a wee dram of Tobermory malt whisky was a secondary attraction for them!

Ally and PC Birkin introduced Jeremy from the BCS. They all listened intently as Jeremy explained in simple terms what fate the white-tailed eagles were facing, and the serious fact that, unless a cure could be administered quickly, white-tailed eagles on Mull could be wiped out in a matter of weeks. There was a look of shock and horror on all of their faces as no one wanted this to happen. There was unanimous support to help these birds but one question came through loud and clear voiced by Donald, a farmer who'd been on Mull all his life. He said, "We all agree but what can we do, we're not vets or mountain climbers, how can we administer these antibiotics?"

Looking around, Callum could see all the farmers gathered nodding their heads in agreement and asking the same question. At that moment Cameron and Emma entered the Mishnish and got nods of recognition and a few "Hello's from the gathered audience. In their hands they were carrying boxes of medicine.

Jeremy said, "We've got a plan to share with you. You are absolutely right, that to try and get some form of direct contact with the birds is going to be impossible, and even if we could time is against us. We simply don't have the man power to do it. We do know, however, that white-tailed eagles do take dead meat and are known to eat dead deer, rabbits and, dare I say it, sheep. Our proposal is to inject the dead sheep with the antibiotics for the white-tailed eagles to eat so that this gets into their systems to cure them."

A deathly hush descended on the Mishnish and Cameron, a frequent visitor, couldn't remember a time when it had been as quiet in the place. For what seemed like an eternity, but in truth was perhaps only ten seconds, no-one said a word and you could have heard a pin drop.

Then, a voice shouted up "And what happens to my lambs when the white-tailed eagles recover. They will have the taste for lamb and will become a nuisance again, and another thing - who'll compensate me for my sheep?"

Jeremy surveyed the pub and could again see some nods of agreement when Ally stepped forward and said:

"You all know me, I have been a farmer all my life and my father before me. In fact, my family have lived on this island for generations. I have been brought up living side by side with the white-tailed eagles and they are one of us – Muileach's. Whatever happens to one happens to us all. This is a period in their lives when they need our help. They have no-one else that they can turn to and it would not be an exaggeration to say that they are looking at extinction on Mull. Now, I haven't told anyone this before, but I truly believe that a white-tailed eagle saved my son's life."

At this point, Ally told the story of how Elgol alerted him to the impending disaster when Callum was stranded in the rowing boat on Loch Ba.

Ally continued, "I, for one, believe that white-tailed eagles have as much right to live on this beautiful Island as you or I. If needs be, I will repay you all for the cost of your sheep out of my own money!"

With the words still echoing round the pub Callum looked around the faces on the farmers as the words started to sink in. Then, Donald, the farmer who had raised the initial concerns, stood up - he was clearly a farmer with experience and someone who commanded the respect of his audience. Callum feared the worst as he opened his mouth to speak:

"That was quite some speech, lad," he said.

He went on, "You all know me, and in the past I haven't been a white-tailed eagle's best friend but I can't imagine life on Mull without them soaring the skies, They're a bit like an annoying neighbour - sometimes they do stuff you don't like but when you need to borrow a hedge-cutter they're always there for you! I haven't an answer as to what happens to my lambs when they've recovered but let's cross that bridge when we come to it. I'm in, what do you want me to do?" he asked.

No sooner had the words left his lips but the mood in the pub lifted and this offer of help was repeated by the assembled mass time and time again.

The noise subsided and Donald shouted up again, "And another thing, you can keep your money Laddie, I speak for us all when I say that we'd be mightily offended if you gave us one penny towards the cost of our sheep." With that, the old farmer gave a menacing look around his fellow farmers daring anyone to speak-up against him and of course, no one did, all nodding in agreement.

Ally couldn't hide the satisfaction on his face and shouted across to Larry the landlord "In that case, Larry, crack open a bottle of your finest Tobermory 15 year-old. Friends, I ask you all to join me in a dram, to the white-tailed eagles!"

They all clambered to the bar to drink to the white-tailed eagles' health.

Before they left, Emma, Jeremy and Cameron briefed everyone as to how to administer the antibiotics into a dead sheep and where best to stake them out on a hillside. All the farmers agreed that they would do this first thing in the morning. They mapped out the whole of the island where they knew the white-tailed eagles nested.

As Cameron, Emma, Ally, Jeremy and Callum left the Mishnish it looked like there were going to be a few more toasts to the white-tailed eagles before the night was done!

As they made their way back to Ally's farm there was a nervous optimism in the Land-rover. They could really now do no more. The rest was up to the farmers to fulfill their side of the bargain and for the white-tailed eagles to take their medicine - the rest would be down to fate.

When they got home, Callum slipped away to go and meet his friends to tell them about the events of the day and to tell Elgol that he had a job to do. He met up with them - told them about the results, the infection, the cure that they'd found, and how they proposed to administer it.

Elgol had lots of questions, "How successful is the antibiotic? How long would it take for them to recover? Would his mum die?"

These were all questions that Callum just couldn't answer. All he could say was "I know this is a worrying time for you Elgol and I'm afraid I haven't got answers to these questions. All I can do is assure you that everyone is doing their best and really they can do no more."

Callum could see the worry still on Elgol's face and whilst the news he'd shared had been good news it didn't take the concern away. Callum thought, "I need to take Elgol's mind off this and get him to do something useful to stop him from worrying."

Callum said to Elgol "You've got a massive job to do tomorrow."

"What's that?" replied Elgol, "What can I do?"

Callum said "Well, first thing in the morning the farmers will all be out on the hillsides staking out the sheep to administer the antibiotics. It will be useless unless the white-tailed eagles eat the meat. Your job is to spread the word and to make sure that all the white-tailed eagles on Mull eat this meat. Even if the white-tailed eagles aren't ill, they need to eat the meat, as it will immunise them from future infection."

Elgol agreed that he would help. Ella also offered her assistance and between them they'd mapped out how they were going to cover the whole island as quickly as they could.

Tomorrow was going to be a very busy day for them all so they all went home to get some rest.

The following morning Elgol was up early with his mum. He could see that she wasn't well but she didn't complain. He told her about the epidemic on Mull that was affecting the white-tailed eagles. She had heard about the two deaths, but put this down to coincidence and had feared poisoning again. Elgol told her that Ally would be putting a dead sheep out on the hills by the loch and that she needed to eat it. Elgol rarely had a cross word with his mother but she wouldn't acknowledge that she was ill - this made him cross.

Elgol left Kilbeg and went to spread the word to the white-tailed eagle families on Mull. They all listened to him and told him they'd think about it, but they were all very nervous about eating dead sheep meat, particularly as it was being staked out in this manner. They knew the dangers of eating poisoned meat. Elgol just hoped that his warning would sink in and that they would take their medicine.

Ella conveyed a similar message but she too, was finding it difficult to get anyone to listen to her – she just hoped that they would.

Back at Callum's home, Ally seemed to have been on the telephone all morning talking to farmers and the police, trying to make sure that things were happening. Later that morning, the nature of the phone calls changed from ones of hope and expectation to ones of despair. He was taking calls from farmers to say that they'd staked the sheep out - white-tailed eagles were circling overhead but they weren't coming down to eat the sheep. These types of calls became more and more frequent - he was at a loss to know what to do next.

He then took a call from Malcolm at Mull boat hire. He'd been following the unfolding story from the start as he had a passion for these birds and also had a vested interest as his livelihood depended on them being successful. There probably wasn't anyone on Mull who knew the birds better.

Jeremy spoke to him and said "Hi Malcolm, our plan to feed the white-tailed eagles with the sheep with antibiotics isn't working at the moment."

Malcolm said, "White-tailed eagles are quite nervous birds and it just may take time for them to get comfortable with eating this "free meat"."

Jeremy said "I hope that's the case - maybe tomorrow will bring better news."

Callum was keeping close to the story and was worried that the plan wasn't working. Clearly Elgol's efforts had been in vain and he needed to get back in touch to let him know the current position.

He met up with them all at the bridge - Elgol and Ella looked exhausted, they'd flown around the whole Island and they were also hungry. Olly and Pollyhannah turned up with a mackerel each and handed them over to Elgol and Ella which they tucked into gratefully.

Whilst they were eating, Callum said "Look, the plan with the sheep isn't working."

Elgol looked so disappointed - all his work and effort had been for nothing and they were no nearer to curing the epidemic. Callum said to Elgol, "Go home and get some rest. My dad won't give up and he'll think of something."

Elgol went home to find his mum waiting for him.

She asked him, "Where have you been?"

Elgol replied "I've been around the island trying to warn the other birds about the serious illness that's affecting white-tailed eagles."

She said "You look exhausted."

Elgol glanced at his mother and she looked awful, her feathers were bedraggled and a couple had fallen out. Her eyes had lost that glint and he was very worried about her. She could see that Elgol was upset and it reminded her of the last time that she'd seen that face when they'd both lost Elgol's father. She wanted to make his pain better so agreed that she would help in any way she could.

Elgol said "The other white-tailed eagles have ignored my warnings and they won't eat the dead sheep. Unless they do, they could catch the disease and die."

Elgol's mum thought for a while and then said to him, "Go back to all the white-tailed eagles from across the island and get them to meet back on the north slope of Benmore at four o clock this afternoon."

Elgol asked his Mum, "Why?" But all she would say was "Don't waste time just get them all there."

Elgol knew better than to argue with his mum so, although he was tired, he had a new lease of life and set off. He started with the closest family at "Tall Trees". He told them that his mother wanted to see them all at Benmore at 4 o'clock - out of respect for Rona they agreed that they would be there. One by one, across the island, they agreed.

Back at Callum's, they were all gathered - PC Birkin, Cameron, Emma, Jeremy and his dad all trying to think how they could solve this problem. There had been another twist in that some of the farmers expressed concern at leaving dead meat on the hillside that could contaminate the land - they felt that unless something happened quickly then they'd be forced to remove the dead sheep. This was another reason why time was against them.

Emma then said "Please bear with me - I want to speak to Malcolm at Mull boat hire, I've got an idea."

Emma had spent quite a lot of time with Malcolm on his boat and had developed a good relationship with him. She came back into the room and said, "Right, we need to get the antibiotics and head for Ulva ferry as quickly as we can - Malcolm is going to take us out down the loch on his boat."

Without questioning Emma's instructions, they quickly gathered their stuff and made their way to the cars and set off to Ulva ferry. Once there, Malcolm was preparing the boat, checking the fuel, loading fishing rods and bringing on board a ruck-sack of binoculars. They got on board and Malcolm headed off towards the loch, all scouring the skies looking for white-tailed eagles.

At Benmore, it was approaching four o'clock and Rona made her way to the North Slope. She looked down and saw the dead sheep staked out below a steep cliff. This brought back memories of her husband and she could picture him lying motionless by a dead sheep. She steeled herself to what was required and as she circled she saw another white-tailed eagle approaching. A few minutes later, more appeared and within the next ten minutes the sky was full of white-tailed eagles - there must have been over forty of them.

On the boat, Callum's keen eyes spotted Rona and then he saw the skies filling with white-tailed eagles, he shouted, "Look, there! The sky is full of white-tailed eagles - what's going on?"

Those in the boat all trained their eyes on the sky above Benmore, "I can't believe it, I haven't seen anything like this before," said Malcolm.

What could they be doing? Malcolm cut the engine to the boat so that they could have a better view of what was happening. After a short period they saw one white-tailed eagle break from the crowd, under his breath Callum said "Go on, Rona, eat the sheep - you can do it?"

Meanwhile, in the sky above Benmore, Elgol had just returned to see his mum swooping down and landing on the rocks by the dead sheep. She moved slowly towards it and, plucking up every ounce of courage that she could muster, started tucking into the dead sheep.

She had a good feed and when she was full she took to the air and encouraged others to go down and feed themselves. It took a while, but slowly, one by one, they started to fly down to the dead sheep.

On the boat, they let out a cheer as they could see what was happening. Emma said "There won't be enough meat for them all - we need to help them."

With that she shouted out her orders to everyone on the boat.

"Callum, you get the rod and catch as many mackerel as you can. Jeremy, when Callum has caught a fish, take it off the line and put it into that bucket. Cameron and I will inject the fish. Ally, you throw the fish off the back of the boat for the white-tailed eagles to catch. Malcolm you keep a steady course alongside Benmore."

They all knew what they had to do and within minutes Ally was throwing the fish off the back of the boat. The white-tailed eagles didn't take long to spot the fish being thrown from the back of Malcolm's boat. At one time or another they had all benefited from Malcolm's generosity in feeding them.

One by one, they started swooping down, skimming the surface with their talons and gracefully picking up the mackerel. Once safe in their talons they would head off to a tree to tuck into their prey. There were a few of the white-tailed eagles that needed more than one attempt and Elgol thought to himself that these must be the ones affected by the midge infection or young ones – allowing him a few moments to think about the time when he was learning to fish.

As Callum looked on, his mind drifted back to his Second World War project and couldn't help but think that this reminded him of the Dambusters' story and how the eagles just looked like the bombers skimming the water. He was soon brought back to the present day when Jeremy bellowed at him "Quick more fish!"

After about fifteen minutes, Emma gave them the bad news that the antibiotics had run out and that by her reckoning there were still around twenty white-tailed eagles that hadn't caught a fish. They could do no more and the only thing they could do was to hope that they would return to their own habitats to feed on the sheep that had been left out for them.

The white-tailed eagles could see that the fish had stopped being thrown and after a few minutes circling, to see if any more would appear, they all headed off in different directions back to their homes. All on the boat watched them disperse and Malcolm headed the boat back to Ulva ferry.

It didn't take them long and as they disembarked they thanked Malcolm for all his help - they all hoped that it would be enough to save the white-tailed eagles.

They met back at Callum's house and all got on the phones to the farmers to tell them what had happened that afternoon. Their spirits were heartened as each of the farmers reported that the white-tailed eagles were back and were feeding on the carcasses - it was working, the treatment plan was working. All they could do now was to hope that the antibiotics would work.

Callum disappeared again down the loch to meet up with his friends. They were all pleased to see one another and delighted that the plan to treat the white-tailed eagles seemed to have worked. They agreed that they would all meet again in a few days time for a progress report, unless that is, anything untoward happened in the meantime. I don't think any of his friends had had a good night's sleep for a while but they certainly all deserved one tonight.

Callum, his dad, Cameron, Jeremy and Emma all spent the next few days keeping an eye on the skies around Mull and as far as they could tell the treatment seemed to be working. The eagles flying seemed to be back to normal and there were no examples of any strange flying or dead white-tailed eagles.

Rona had soon started to feel better, so much so, that she did a lap of the island to check on the other families for herself.

She told them all how much the farmers had helped them and they all agreed that they would not take a lamb ever again as a way of paying back the farmers.

In the meantime, as lamb was now firmly off the menu they would have to eat more fish, so as a thank you to Malcolm, they all agreed to take it in turns to put on a show for Malcolm's Mull white-tailed eagle boat trips so that his trips would remain full - they set up a rota with Elgol, Ella and Rona leading the way.

Before Emma and Jeremy left Mull to go back to their regular jobs, Ally invited all the farmers and everyone involved in the rescue to a Ceilidh in Salen to say thank you. Franky, the ferryman was now Franky the accordion man, leading the dancing, and everyone had a wonderful time even if there were a few sore heads and tired legs the next day.

Emma and Jeremy would certainly never forget their trip to Mull and vowed to return next year. In fact, it looks like there could have been romance in the air as Callum overheard Emma and Jeremy making plans to see each other when they both got back to Glasgow!

The following day, Callum got together with his friends, mightily relieved that the crisis had been averted, and they all agreed that it would be great to now enjoy a long quiet summer. Before they swam off, Olly and Pollyhannah confessed to the fact that, purely for medicinal reasons, they'd both caught and eaten a mackerel each thrown from the back of Malcolm's boat and as a result they didn't fear catching this disease either!

91307216R00117

Made in the USA
Columbia, SC
19 March 2018